KU-240-266

DEVILISH CHARM

KASEY MARTIN

WITHDRAWN FROM STOCK
COUNTY LIBRARY

Jessica Watkins Presents

WITHDRAWN FROM
COUNTY LIBRARY STOCK

COPYRIGHT

Copyright © 2017 by Kasey Martin
Published by Jessica Watkins Presents

All rights reserved, including the right of reproduction in whole or in part in any form. Without limiting the right under copyright reserved above, no part of this publication may be reproduced, stored in or introduced into a retrieval system, or transmitted, in any form by means (electronic, mechanical, photocopying, recording, or otherwise), without the prior written permission of the copyright owner.

This is a work of fiction. Names, characters, places and incidents are either the product of the author's imagination or are used fictitiously, and any resemblance to actual persons, living or dead, business establishments, events, or locales, is entirely coincidental.

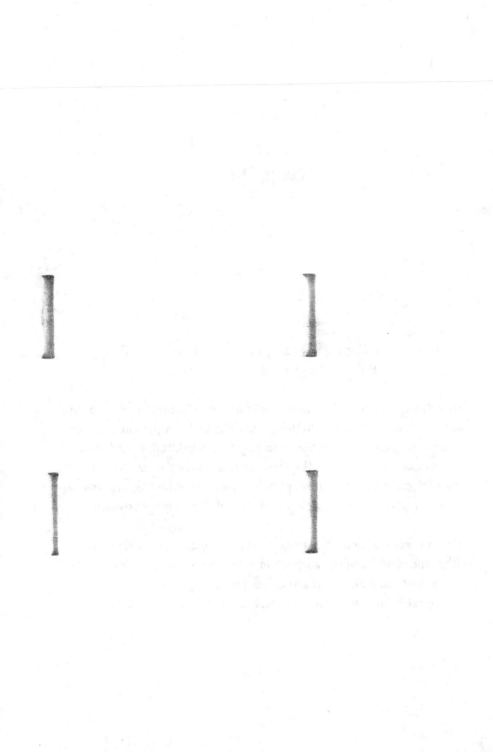

Chapter One

FARREN

"This is your girl, Farren, and as usual I'm your ride or die chick for K105 the Jam on your mid-morning commute. As usual, I'm gonna take a break from our regular scheduled program to play a little old school Biggie for ya'll, and we'll be taking caller number one hundred and five for the chance to win tickets to our annual Jam Fest. Alright D.J. Smooth, drop that beat!"

"Uh-ha, it's all good baby bay-bee, uh... It was all a dream..."

Farren smiled and nodded to the beat of one of her all-time favorite songs. Music was her life, it was in her blood, in her soul, and she loved it. As a little girl growing up, she knew she wanted to be a musician. First, she tried singing, and although her passion was there, she couldn't hold a tune in a bucket if she tried. Next, she tried her hand at being in the marching band; again, her many talents did not extend to playing a musical instrument either. Lastly, she tried her hand at rapping, and although she wasn't winning any cyphers, she was pretty good. Farren later put her knack for clever word play into hosting the

Leabharlanna Fhine Ga

battles which led to experimenting with mixed tapes and DJing gigs, and now she had her own mid-morning radio show.

Farren Bell had worked her ass off to get where she was, and she had to pay her dues like everyone else. She made her way up from lowly intern to have her very own show, although having her own show was a result of her former co-host double crossing her and stealing her chance at a nationally syndicated show. But sometimes, that's just the way things were, so instead of wallowing in self-pity, she looked at it as a blessing and pushed forward.

Her former co-host was a real snake, but she was glad not to have to work with him any longer. After he had left, the station got a new program director, and things were starting to look up. However, the new director, Evan Clarke was just another headache that Farren had to deal with.

At first, Farren just overlooked his condescending tone. After all, she had worked three years with her former co-host Dave Bryson, but Evan's snide remarks and narrowed icy stares started to get to her more and more each day.

Farren wasn't sure what Evan's problem was, but after six months of his bull, she was about ready to go off. However, this was her career, and although it was an unconventional workplace, she still carried the burden of being one of the few African American females there, so she felt the need to destroy the ghetto stereotype that people thought about black women. Popping off in the workplace wasn't in her best interest.

"So Farren, are you ready for the Jam Fest this year?" a deep and melodic voice questioned.

Farren smiled up at DJ Smooth. They had been working together for the past year, and he was fine as hell, but she didn't mix business with pleasure. Her grandma always told her, "Baby you never shit where you eat." For years, Farren didn't know what that meant until she made the mistake of sleeping with a co-worker, the situation turned messy quick, and she knew exactly what her grandma Daisy meant.

"Yeah, I'm ready. There are some great acts this year, so it should be fun," Farren responded with a smile. Her and Smooth often talked during commercial breaks, and while the music played, it was an easy way to pass the time.

"I'm shocked at all of the hip-hop acts that were invited. I wonder what changed their minds. I had to fight for a measly two songs to be added to the playlist, and now they are just adding rappers all willy nilly." Smooth's deep chocolate complexion lit up with his broad, dimpled smile. His brown eyes twinkled with mirth.

Farren laughed, but Smooth was right. This was a pop station first, a rock station next with a little rap thrown in, but this year there were more hip-hop acts than there ever was before. Farren appreciated the change, but she recognized the fact that today's rap was more mainstream.

"Well, to be fair, the artists they added aren't hardcore hip-hop. They're more MC Hammer than Tupac."

They both laughed at the reference. Both of them knew that the rappers that were set to perform were more bubble gum pop than Taylor Swift, but that was what the fans wanted, so that was what they gave them. Not that there was anything wrong with bubble gum music, but it just wasn't real hip-hop.

"So, I heard you have to do a live show with the Solomon Kings. What's up with that?" Smooth asked, his brows furrowed in question.

"Yeah, I think maybe the higher-ups are trying to show the diversity in the station or something." Farren shrugged. She figured the resident pop/hip-hop DJ interviewing a rock band was their idea of diversity. "They are a cool band though, so it shouldn't be all that bad."

"I'll take your word for it. There's only so much of that rock shit I can take."

"Aww, come on Smooth, you can't possibly tell me you're a musical snob. I appreciate all types of music. Music is good for the soul." Farren smiled, showing her perfect white teeth.

Smooth chuckled. "I'm not a snob. But you can't tell me you like country music?"

"Of course, I like country music. I'm from Texas."

"Bullshit! I'm from Texas too, and I hate all that cryin'... my wife left me, my truck was stolen, and my dog died... ole sad woe is me ass songs."

Farren laughed loudly. "Come on, Smooth, not all country music is like that. You need to give it a chance."

"Nah, I'm good."

They laughed and chatted throughout the rest of the show, and before long it was time to go. The playlist Farren had to work with was one she enjoyed, and playing music she liked always made her day easy. Farren was packing up her things and getting ready to head out when suddenly her day went from pleasant to poop in five seconds flat.

"I need you in my office before you leave." Evan walked away without even bothering to hear Farren's response to his command.

What a colossal douche!

————

"You beckoned, oh gracious one?" Farren sarcastically bowed as she entered Evan's office.

"You're not funny, Farren." Evan turned with his usual glare reserved especially for her.

When Farren first met Evan, she thought he was attractive. He was tall with a lean muscular physique, a head full of blonde hair, and the prettiest blue eyes. But even his good looks couldn't disguise the fact that he was an ultimate ass.

"What do you need, Evan? I was on my way out." Farren took a seat in front of his desk, and Evan's face remained serious.

Farren didn't know what he could possibly want, but she wished he would've just sent it in an email because she hated being in the same room with him for too long. He always gave her the impression that she was somehow beneath him.

"The Solomon Kings are a very important band. They will be huge stars soon, and we need to have a good working relationship with these guys. It's pertinent that you keep that in mind when you're conducting your live broadcast."

Farren kept her expression blank, but inside boiling hot lava was fighting to come out. If she could spit fire at his head in that moment, she would. Farren took her job seriously, and although she had fun, she was the constant professional. She was the last one he needed to remind of the importance of her job. Especially since the last time they worked a concert together, Evan was the one snuggling up to groupies and forgetting his job.

"I know how to do my job, Evan. I've never done anything to suggest otherwise." Farren's voice was low and without emotion. She wouldn't give him the satisfaction of getting loud.

Evan narrowed his eyes before responding. "I just want to make sure we're clear on the expectations we have for the interview."

"Crystal clear. Is that all?" Farren began to rise out of her chair, and gathered her things before he could respond. She was halfway to the door before he spoke.

"I'll be joining you for the interview. You know, in case you need any help." Evan smirked.

Farren nodded and kept walking. Evan knew that she hated being treated like she was some newcomer that had no idea how to do her job. He had been riding her a lot lately, dropping in unexpectedly on her shows, critiquing every little thing she did and said, even checking over her playlists, which he had never done in the past. None of her directors did.

Most program directors she'd had just let her get on and do her job. They trusted that she was capable, and they knew she would get the job done. But Evan was the exact opposite and he was getting worse.

Maybe it's time for me to start looking at other stations, Farren thought solemnly as she made her way to her car. She had proven herself time and time again, and to be treated like she didn't know what she was doing after seven years was more than insulting—it was downright disrespectful. But Farren could only hope he was using her as an excuse so he could party with the band and not look like he was a fanboy.

As Farren was walking to her car, her cell rang. She was going to just deny the call until she caught a glimpse of the name. Her best friend, Eden Lancaster always knew when to call.

"Hey E-boogie, what's shakin' bacon?" Farren answered with as much cheer as she could muster.

"Hey Ms. Bell." Eden paused before continuing, "You sound weird. What's going on with you?"

"Same ole' work stuff, you know how it is." Farren tried to sound nonchalant, but she knew before the words even fully left her lips, her friend wouldn't let it slide.

"It's that punk, Evan isn't it? I swear I can get Eddie to beat him up if he's being a jerk again." Eden offered up her bodyguard's services like he was a hit man instead of someone that provided her with security.

Farren couldn't help the lighthearted giggle that came out. She loved Eden. They had been besties since they were in second grade, and they were always there for one another no matter what.

"I don't think I will be needing Eddie's services quite yet. By the way, I don't think your bodyguard or your boyfriend would appreciate you hiring him out." Farren scoffed.

"You know if I told Camedon how that dick, Evan, was treating you, he would kick his ass himself."

"Yeah, you're right." Farren smiled to herself then sobered once she thought about her last conversation.

"Why don't you come out for a drink tonight? You don't work tomorrow, right?"

"I could use a drink." Farren wanted to get started on her search for a potential new gig. It was always good to have options in life, especially if you found yourself unsatisfied with your current predicament. But she could always use a night of drinks and fun with her friend, and start a new day with a clear head.

"So, what do you say? Uber it over to my house around eight we'll get dolled up, and go twerk a little somethin'. I think a little alcohol and dancing might give you your happy back," Eden sassily suggested.

"You know what? You're absolutely right. Drinks and dancing is exactly what I need. I'll see you around eight with my best get em' girl dress on and ready to go."

"That's my girl. Make sure you wear your best fuck me heels too. Maybe you can catch a man and he can dust out that cave... it could only help you." Eden cackled loudly.

"Wait a damn minute. How you just gone have me out here in these streets? And who said I need anything dusted? Just cause' you got a man now doesn't mean you can act brand new like you don't know I keep a maintenance man on lock."

"Girl, bye. We both know you ain't gettin' any. Let's not pretend that your last 'maintenance man' was Erick, and his slick ass been out the picture."

Farren was *not* about to admit that everything Eden said was true. She hadn't had sex in months, but Erick wasn't all bad. He introduced her to Club Euphoria before Eden even knew what it was. Not that Farren would ever divulge that little secret.

"Whatever, heffa," Farren said, effectively ending the unwanted conversation.

"I'll see you this evening." Farren could hear Eden laughing as she disconnected the call. Tonight, she was determined to have a good time before making any life changing decisions.

Chapter Two

JONES

Jones Sullivan was a man on the verge and dealing with his crazy ass work schedule was quickly pushing him closer to the edge of the cliff. The last couple of months had been strained between him and almost everyone in his life. After the fiasco at Club Euphoria, the club he owned with his best friend, Jones slowly pulled away from everybody, drowning himself in work. He had been avoiding Cam the most, but he just couldn't face him.

Jones felt responsible that someone he considered family tried to extort money from him and Camedon. It was an elaborate revenge plot that Jones inadvertently played a part in. If he would've been more careful, nobody would've been able to get so close. Jones was reckless, and it endangered the people around him, especially Cam.

His cell phone ringing brought him out of his thoughts.

Jones saw that it was Camedon, who had been calling him constantly. If he continued to ignore his calls, Jones would get an unwanted visitor. So, to keep that from happening, he answered.

"Hello."

"Hey, Sullivan. Nice of you to answer my damn call, finally. Let me guess, you're busy?" The snide remarks couldn't hide the worry in his best friend's voice, and it made Jones feel even more like shit.

"We have a company together, so *you* know how busy I am."

"Busy, right. I know your ass has been avoiding me. What the hell, man?"

Jones' sigh came out in a loud huff. "Man, I just got stuff on my mind. That's all."

"Bullshit. How long have we've known each other? I know when you're going through something. I also know when to give you space, and when to put a foot up your ginger ass."

"Fuck you, slick asshole. My hair is NOT red, it's auburn." Jones chuckled. Camedon was the only one that could ever get away with that ginger bullshit. He was also the only one that could bring him out of his funk by telling him what he needed to hear.

"Like I said, ginger. Now, whatever you're going through, it's time you and me have a conversation. Tonight," Camedon said with finality. Jones wasn't in the habit of letting anybody tell him shit, but he owed his friend an explanation.

"Alright. When and Where?"

"Meet me at my house around eight. We'll talk when you get here."

"Cool, see you in a few." Jones disconnected the call and he knew that he would have to get his thoughts together before they had this much needed conversation.

Jones wasn't the type of man to wallow in self-pity, and he wasn't going to do that now. But this situation wasn't like anything he had ever dealt with before. He was a man that took what he wanted, controlled everything around him, and didn't give a damn about what anybody had to say.

He had to get back to the man that he was. The talk with Camedon would help him get past some of the guilt he held. Jones knew he had to let it go, and move on with his life. He hadn't even gone to Euphoria to party. If he could avoid it all together, he would. But it was one of his biggest earners out of all his businesses. And no matter what was going on around him, Jones was not a failure in business, and he would never allow that to happen.

It was another few hours before Jones headed out to Camedon's house. Camedon's building wasn't too far from his, so it only took a couple of minutes to get there. Laughter caught Jones' attention as he strolled into the lobby of the building. He stopped in his tracks at the melodic sound, and that was when he caught a glimpse of the beauty that haunted his dreams. Eden and her best friend, Farren were getting into a vehicle. Even though he was standing a good distance away, and her back was to him, there was no mistaking those voluptuous curves of Farren Bell.

With just a glimpse, his whole body reacted. He could feel his temperature rise, his body heating, and his pulse picked up speed. Jones had never in his adult life responded to a woman in this manner. His thing was to conquer and move on without a second thought. But that would never be the case with Farren Bell, especially after seeing her only once. Jones had obsessed over Farren, and when he finally met her, it was then that he realized that she would be part of his life. Just not in the way he fantasized about.

Because Farren was now part of his circle of friends, that made her different from other women. And Jones' reputation preceded him, so their one-on-one contact had been limited. He would have to give her the time she needed to get used to him.

He would slowly wear her down; he would talk to her and get to know her, something Jones never did with any woman. But she was worth it because once he had her, and he would eventually, he would never let her go.

But before he could think about his pursuit of Farren, Jones had to talk with Camedon to clear the air. However, as soon as he got his shit together, he would focus on getting what he wanted... Farren Bell.

————

Jones sauntered into Camedon's penthouse apartment. It was time to handle up and get back on track. He found Camedon lounging in the living room sipping on a drink. Jones went directly to the bar and poured himself some whiskey, and joined his friend.

"So, what's on your mind, Sullivan? You've been looking like shit and acting even worse."

"Well, damn. No need to be kind in your friend's time of need." Jones chuckled, taking a drink.

"Whatever, you can try to play that sensitive shit with somebody else," Camedon shook his head, "but not me."

Jones took a deep breath. "I know man. I've just been feeling responsible for all the stuff that went down. If it wasn't for me... I was reckless, and arrogant."

"Look, dude, we were young. And everyone is a little arrogant at twenty something. But we can't live our lives thinking about things we should've done. You'll drive yourself crazy. It's in the past, and you have to let that shit go."

Jones nodded. "Logically, of course I know that. But I just can't shake the feeling that I've could've done more. It would've saved a lot of people a lot of trouble."

"Indeed. But all we can do is learn from the lesson and not repeat our mistakes."

"You're right." Jones couldn't argue with Cam's point.

"We've did the best we could, and now we're better for it."

After everything that happened, the security measures they put into place were the best. Nobody would be able to get close enough to harm anybody in his life ever again. Jones was determined to protect those around him. If he could help it, he would never drop the ball again.

"But it was a lot of shit that could've been avoided. It just doesn't sit right with me."

"Yeah. I felt some guilt myself getting Eden involved in all of it. I know exactly how you feel. But things happened the way they did for a reason. I'll be forever grateful that Eden forgave me, and we are stronger now."

Jones nodded his understanding.

"You have to get past the bullshit, and get back to yourself, man. All that crap is history. You have to let it go and move on." Camedon looked at Jones with a serious expression.

"I know, you're right. I just needed time to get out of my head," Jones replied.

"I'm glad you know I'm right." Camedon smirked. "So, now that we've got all that sensitive shit out the way, can you come back to the club? It hasn't been the same there without you, and your playmates have been hounding the hell out of me. I thought Eden was going to snatch one of them up last week." Camedon laughed.

Jones laughed at the image of petite Eden trying to snatch anyone up, but he wouldn't put it past her. She was quite the feisty little thing. "Why was Eden trying to fight?"

"You know how Euphoria is. The women were a little too friendly when asking about you, rubbing on my chest and giggling. It didn't help that they were half naked or in some cases, completely naked."

Jones laughed loudly. "I'm completely shocked she didn't slap the hell out of them if that was the case."

"I know, right. My woman looks nice and timid, but don't let that fool you. She's all fire." Camedon winked as he chuckled.

Jones caught the double entendre. Although he and Camedon swapped sexual escapades in the past, his friend wouldn't dare talk about the love of his life with anyone. He would never disrespect Eden like that, and Jones would kick his ass if he even thought about it.

"Well, I still don't think I'll be partying at Euphoria anytime soon." Jones looked at the narrow-eyed glare of his best friend and he knew that this conversation was far from over.

"After we just put all this shit to rest, you still don't want to party?" Camedon's face had confusion written all over it. "Did you take a vow of celibacy? Do you have a girlfriend I don't know about?"

Jones almost choked on his drink when he mentioned girlfriend. He admitted to himself that his ongoing obsession with a certain curvy beauty was one of the reasons he hadn't been up to his usual shenanigans with his playmates, but he decided to keep that information to himself.

"No, to all of the above. With everything that's happened, I realized that I can't keep doing the same stuff. All the different women..." Jones trailed off. "I know we put more security measures in place for the club, but the freedom just isn't there for me anymore."

"I understand, man. If you need to change, I'm here for you, and I get it."

Jones nodded. "I can't keep doing the same things expecting different results. It's time I grew up."

"We all have to at some point." Camedon raised his glass, and they clinked them together.

Jones still loved Euphoria and the sexual freedom it represented. But going from woman to woman seeking that thrill through attention just wasn't what he wanted anymore. The thrill he sought came from the attention of one woman. And he intended to have it.

After Farren's night out with Eden, she felt a little more relaxed. She wasn't going to let Evan run her off her job, plus she still had her fashion blog *Curvy Girl Swag*, but she decided that looking for another station to work for was a good idea.

Farren thought back on her girl's night out. She could always count on her bestie to keep her grounded.

"Now tell me what douche extraordinaire did now..." Eden demanded as only she could.

"Evan was just being his usual shitty self." Farren waved it off not wanting to get into details. It would only serve to piss her off.

"Well, if you don't want to talk about work, which is the reason we came out," Eden gave her the side-eye, and Farren couldn't help but to snicker. "Order another drink, so you can at least relax.

Farren agreed and quickly ordered another drink as she bobbed her head to the hip-hop music that was playing. Eden had gotten a prime spot in the downtown club that they frequently patronized, they could see the dancefloor, the DJ, and were close to the bar. It was an excellent location for people watching, and when they wanted to dance, they didn't have to fight the crowd.

Both Eden and Farren were sipping their drinks when Farren's new favorite song Crew by Goldlink started playing. Without hesitation, she pulled Eden to the floor.

She see money all around me... I look like I'm the man, yeah...

Farren was grooving when she felt someone at her back. Now every woman knows not to turn around instantly. The first reason is the guy could be the bugaboo you don't want to make eye contact with or you will never get rid of his ass, reason two is you could seem to desperate and no man wants a thirsty chick. So, you rely on your bestie to check out the guy for you and give the subtle nod yes, or shake no.

So, when Eden's eyes went wide, and she turned away, Farren was confused as hell. So Farren did a shimmy twist with a little head nod to catch a glance at who was behind her. And low and behold if it wasn't the old man with the gold teeth, and track suit.

Every club has one, the player that just won't turn in his card. Farren could do nothing but laugh and keep dancing. She wouldn't be dusting out any caves, but she had to admit Jeromey Rome had some moves on him, so they stayed on the floor shaking their groove thing for the rest of the night.

———

Farren smiled at her thoughts as she looked out at the gathering audience. She had an interview to do with the Solomon Kings, and by the looks of the rowdy crowd, she knew it was going to be a long night. Farren had been preparing for the concert all month, the exhaustion was finally kicking in, and she was dead on her feet.

"Hey, there Farren." She automatically turned when she heard her name, and when Farren saw who the speaker was, she instantly regretted turning around so quick.

"What are you doing here?" Farren questioned as she looked the slimy man up and down in disgust. She hadn't seen his shady ass in forever, and she wasn't happy that she had to lay eyes on him now.

"Aww, Princess Farren isn't still butt hurt that I got the job she wanted? Get over it already." He chuckled snidely.

Farren didn't hate many people, but Dave Bryson was a low down dirty weasel that deserved every bit of venom Farren could muster to throw his way. Dave was her former co-host of the mid-morning radio show, and the very snake that stole her opportunity to go nationwide.

Farren didn't respond. She just looked at him with fire blazing in her golden-brown eyes.

"So, are you mute now? You normally have some sassy come back. Is your black girl magic all used up?" he questioned with a smirk.

That did it. Farren had no patience for Dave and his bullshit. "You know what you little snake, you did me a favor by leaving. My ratings boosted as soon as you slithered your whack ass away. Let's be real, you got that job because of nepotism, and we both know it. You are a nonfactor, my show is way more successful now, so fuck you and the horse you rode in on. How's that for black girl magic, bitch." Her calm voice belied the seething rage held just below the surface. Farren was closer than she'd ever been to committing assault.

Dave's pale face turned red with indignation. His mouth flapped open and closed but without a snappy retort.

Farren didn't wait for him to respond. Her lip twitched up involuntarily in an angry snarl as she turned and headed away from her nemesis. She had to play nice, grin and bear the insults, and turn a blind's eye to jerks all because she was an African-American woman that worked at a predominantly white business. She always had to be extra diligent to *not* help perpetuate the stereotypes of black women in the workplace. But today was not the day for nice.

"Not today, Satan," Farren mumbled to herself as she made her way from the screaming rock fans towards the back of the venue. She was not about to go to jail behind Dave's ignorant ass.

She weaved her way to a vendor selling beers. She wasn't technically working yet, and the radio station encouraged having a good time. Although she usually wouldn't partake in alcohol, she needed something to take the edge off. The line was hella long, but she would suffer through it to calm her nerves.

Farren was distracted checking her phone, so when someone touched her on the lower back, she was startled. She jumped and whirled around ready to punch the holy hell out of whoever had the audacity to put their hands on her.

"Whoa there, Tyson." Evan laughed, but his blue eyes had their usual glare.

Farren sneered at him. She didn't know why he was laughing because she didn't see anything funny. Evan's presence just made her mood worse, and this night had been super irritating already. Farren's natural happy-go-lucky attitude was nowhere to be found.

She stepped away from his touch. "You scared the crap outta me!"

"I'm not sure why you're so jumpy but you need to calm down. This is an important interview."

"I know how important this interview is. I've been here for a while, and I've already set up." Farren raised her brows in challenge.

"As long as you know how important it is, and make sure you do your job." Evan sauntered away like he ruled the world, and Farren was glad he left before she got the chance to respond.

She decided that she'd had enough of dealing with assholes for one night, so she took a deep breath and ordered her beer. She was going to do her job and go home.

After getting her drink, Farren made her way to the front of the venue. She sipped her beer as she stood off the main stage where the Solomon Kings were playing. They were a new band that had a loyal following, and they were on the verge of blowing up on the rock scene. She had to interview them for the station's social media page, and then she was out. Evan had disappeared yet again, but she wouldn't worry about where he was. She just didn't want him popping up and getting on her nerves in the middle of the interview.

Farren was getting ready to do her interview when Evan finally showed up with some blonde bimbo hanging off his arm. She knew that he was just using the interview as an excuse to get close to the band, and more importantly their groupies. He made it seem like he was there because she was incompetent, when all along he just wanted to get laid. Farren rolled her eyes at Evan's behavior.

"Farren, are you ready yet? We need to get this show on the road," Evan barked as if he were running the entire show.

"You would know that *I've* been ready to go if you were here to actually work."

Evan's big boss façade faded, and he squinted his bright blue eyes at her. "Don't question me."

"That was clearly a statement... not a question," came Farren's snarky response. She had been in bitch mode since her run-in with Dave, and she couldn't seem to turn it off. Technically Evan wasn't her boss, but he did have input with the radio heads in charge of her show. She should really try to be nice, but tonight it just wasn't in her.

He had glared at her before he turned his attention back to Botox Barbie. Evan leaned down and whispered something in her ear before the bimbo giggled, thrust her boobs out, and looked around the open space. Farren noted that the woman must be in groupie heaven with all the testosterone and rock stars floating around the large room. Farren took a deep breath and rolled her eyes as Evan exited practically dragging the groupie from her paradise.

Fish, the lead singer of the band, came over for his interview. "We really appreciate you doing this DJ Farren." His voice was a smooth baritone and he had a southern drawl, and a wicked smile.

Farren had to admit that Fish was pretty cute for a rocker type. He was tall but not lanky, and his body had a nice build but not packed with muscle. His warm brown eyes framed by thick lashes gave him an almost innocent look, but the mischievous glint in them gave him that bad boy appeal that most rockers had.

"You can just call me Farren." She smiled at him with a wink. DJ'ing was her job, not her name. She never came up with a clever name; she was merely Farren.

Fish gave her an even sexier smile, and Farren noticed not for the first time that this guy had a little more swag than she gave him credit for.

Farren finished up the interview with the band and was packing up her gear. She noticed that Evan still hadn't made his way back for the actual work, but she was done, and getting the hell out of there. She slung her bag over her shoulder and was heading toward the exit when one of the assistants from the station ran towards her looking frazzled.

"Farren! Oh my gosh, I'm so happy to see you. Have you seen Evan? He was supposed to give me passes for tomorrow's show for some VIPs, but I can't find him!"

"Sarah, calm down. I haven't seen him, but I have some passes. They're in my car. I'll run and get them."

"Thanks so much, Farren! You're a life saver!" Sarah excitedly responded.

Farren smiled and headed to her car. She'd parked on the far side of the venue, but if she cut through an alley, she could get there and back within a few minutes. Farren got to her car and back to hand the passes off to Sarah in record time.

On the way back, she decided she would take the shortcut back through the alley so she could make it home in time for her favorite show and a glass of wine. Farren quickly walked behind the building through a couple of parked cars and headed toward the alley. The closer she got to the entrance, she heard what she thought was a scuffle. She really didn't want to turn around and go all the way back around the building to get to her car. It was probably just a couple of drunk concert goers, so she decided to proceed with caution.

Farren walked slowly and quietly, so hopefully, the drunks wouldn't notice her. She saw two rather large men not just scuffling but full on fighting. *Shit! I'm not walking through that*, Farren thought as she slid closer to the wall to hide in the shadows. Suddenly, one of the men got the upper hand. He put his opponent in a chokehold. The other man was gasping, but the other guy didn't let up.

The man with the upper hand made a move so fast that Farren didn't know what happened until the other man slumped to the ground holding his neck. The man casually wiped a blade on the other man's pants as he lay on the ground making a gurgling sound.

Farren's eyes were wide in disbelief. *Did he just slash his throat?* She crouched down low behind a dumpster and prayed the man didn't come her way to leave the alley. She peeked out to see if the murderer was gone, but the man was dragging the other guy further in the shadows in her direction.

Shit! Farren sunk lower making herself as small as possible. She heard the man stop a few feet away from her when she heard a cell phone ring. She gasped thinking it was hers, but she didn't move.

"The fuck?" The man's voice was rough and gravelly. Farren could hear his footsteps nearing closer to her hiding spot. However, it was his phone that had gone off, and it was ringing again, gaining his attention.

Before she knew it, the man was walking right past her, his focus on the phone call. He turned slightly, and the street light hit his face just right. Farren had never in her life seen this man, but his eyes were a haunting pale blue, and his face was not one she would ever forget. He turned around once more before he stalked off out of the alley.

Farren was afraid to move, fearing that the man would still be lurking around and see her come out of the alley, so she sat frozen in her spot. Tears were streaming down her face when she finally decided it was time to get up and get the hell out of there. Farren took a deep breath and headed in the opposite direction of the killer. She moved as quickly and as quietly as possible, checking behind her every few seconds.

Holy Shit! I just witnessed a murder!

Once she made it to the other end of the alley, Farren took off as fast as her legs would carry her. She was almost in a full sprint when she ran into what she thought was a brick wall. She bounced back, and she was sure that the fall was going to hurt like hell, but strong arms wrapped around her body and kept her from falling.

"Farren?" The deep voice was familiar, and she was both incredibly shocked and relieved to see the man standing in front of her.

"Oh my God! I'm so glad to see you!" Farren wrapped her arms around him and let the tears flow down her face.

CHAPTER FOUR

JONES

Fifteen minutes earlier...

Jones sat listening to the radio in his G-Wagon Sport. He couldn't believe he let his knuckleheaded little brother talk him into going to a rock concert of all things. He promised himself he would stop being so distant from his family.

Jones was baby number four out of seven. He was the quintessential middle child, wanting attention and acting out, which explained some of his exhibitionist tendencies. But even with his eccentric ways, he was closest to his youngest brother, Jasper, and his older brother, Jax.

Jax, the fixer of the family, was Jones' exact opposite. Jax was always cool, calm, and collected. He blended into the background with ease, and fixed any problems by any means necessary. He wasn't big on extra attention, and was known as the silent, brooding one.

Then there was his youngest brother, Jasper who was the typical party boy. He was always into shit, but he knew how to make any bad situation better. And like Jones, Jasper was able to charm just about anyone, which was why Jones found himself outside a concert venue waiting for his brother instead of being home relaxing with a beer.

Jones knew that his youngest brother, Jasper was up to no good as usual, but he wouldn't leave until he at least got a text from him. Then, the shrill ring of his cell echoed throughout the quiet interior. Jones checked the caller id, and he knew he was going to have to cuss his brother out.

"You little shit, where the hell are you?" Jones' tone was gruff and full of exasperation.

"Hello to you too, bro. I ran into some construction on I35, so I'm running a little late."

Jones pulled the phone away from his ear and looked at the screen in disbelief. At that moment, he wanted to pull his brother through the phone and punch him directly in the throat. I35 had been under construction for over twenty years. His brother must be high if he thought that excuse was going to fly.

"I know damn well you didn't just give me that lame ass excuse. You must want me to kick your little ass?"

Jasper chuckled, but Jones didn't find shit funny. There was plenty he could've been doing on a Thursday night. His phone flashed with a message from one of his old playmates, Lindsey, and sighed. *Plenty I could be doing*, he thought, more than a little irritated, but he had decided to hang out with his brother instead.

"I'm serious, bro." Jasper broke into Jones' thoughts with his comment. "The roadworks switched, so I got turned around. I'm about fifteen minutes away."

"Fine, but if your little punk ass ain't here in fifteen minutes, I'm out." Jones disconnected the call before his brother had time to reply.

Jones Sullivan was the middle child in a large family. He had six brothers and one sister. His parents apparently wanted a girl since they stopped after Jennifer was born. His large Irish-American family was unconventional at best, and downright savage at worst.

Jones sat back to relax for a minute before he left his brother high and dry. Even though he hadn't been partying at Euphoria, he could've easily answered the call from Lindsey. But lately, it just wasn't in him.

After Jones was used as a part of a blackmail scheme, he decided that he should slow down on his philandering ways. These days he went to the club for business rather than pleasure, but he couldn't help thinking back to the one night that had an unexpected effect on him. He let his mind drift back to that night, a night that he would never forget—the night he first laid his eyes on a voluptuous, brown-eyed beauty.

The viewing room was set up for comfort with large sofas and chairs facing each of the two-way mirrors. Jones sat in the middle of the room alone. He was normally the exhibitionist, loving the attention of having sex in public. Not often, but sometimes he would give into his voyeuristic tendencies, and end up here, watching.

She was completely bare; her cinnamon brown complexion seemed to shimmer with her every move. Jones could tell by the look in her honey brown eyes that she was a woman that loved to be watched. He tracked her every move as she ran her hands down her body, generous with curves. She was tall, and her legs seem to be never-ending, but she wasn't the waif-like body type Jones usually preferred. A woman. Her round hips and full breasts called to him like no other woman ever had. She slid her hand to the most intimate of places. Her eyes seemed to look directly into Jones'. He knew that it was impossible because there was no way she could see him through the two-way mirror, but he couldn't stop the urge of wanting to devour her. She continued to touch herself, her hands dipping into her wetness as she bit her plump lip. She squeezed and caressed her own breasts as she began to pant. Jones couldn't take his eyes off of her, his cock growing impossibly hard in his trousers as she moaned and panted, bringing herself to climax. He groaned out loud at the sound.

Jones ran his hand through his light auburn hair. He never would've expected to see his mystery woman again, but the joke was on him. Not only did he see her again, but he also met her face to face, and she had absolutely no idea who he was.

Jones' cell phone chimed, he looked down and saw that his brother was close, so with a heavy sigh, he exited his vehicle. Jones hit the key fob and locked his car. He turned and started towards the venue, strolling casually and checking his messages when out of the corner of his eye, he saw a body barreling toward him.

He turned just in time to have a curvaceous beauty slam into his muscled chest. Before she could fall, he reached his arms out and grabbed her. Without a second thought as to what he was doing, he pulled her close to his body.

Jones never would've guessed that his salacious thoughts would've manifested themselves and crash into him. He finally had her in his arms, but when he looked into her gorgeous round face, he saw something that he never again wanted to see grace her features... terror.

———

"Farren?" His voice was filled with concern. *Why in the hell is she running?* Jones couldn't help looking around for whoever he had to beat the shit out of for scaring her.

"Oh my God! I'm so glad to see you!" Farren wrapped her arms around him, and he noticed that she was crying.

"Farren, sweetheart. What's wrong?" Jones tried his best to remain calm. Crying women weren't his forte, but he was quickly noticing that Farren Bell took him right out of his comfort zone every single time they came into contact.

"Jones, please. You've got... gotta get me ou... out of here. Ple... please." She begged him through hiccups and tears. He could barely make out what she was saying.

"Okay, sweetie. Just calm down for me, can you do that?" He tried to make his voice calm, but the panic she was displaying put him on high alert. He continued to scan the parking lot as he held her trembling body close.

"I just saw a murder." Her voice was so small that he barely understood what she said.

"I'm sorry I must've heard you wrong. Did you say you just saw a murder?" Jones questioned in disbelief as he looked down into her flushed face.

She took a shuddering breath. "Ye-yes." She shook her head vehemently. "I saw a murder. We need to call the police. Please, Jones."

Jones didn't know what to make of the situation. Farren was far from a damsel in distress or frantic. Every time he'd seen her, she'd been cool, calm, and collected. So, if she believed that she saw someone killed, then he was inclined to believe her.

"Alright, just take a deep breath." He cupped her face in his large hands and looked deep into her eyes. Her chest moved up and down as she followed his directions. He couldn't help but notice her plump bottom lip that was slightly larger than her top one. He found himself consumed with wanting to kiss the fear from her eyes.

Jones leaned down, ready to take her lips in a passionate kiss when he heard a loud bang. Farren jumped and clutched his shirt tight as she rammed her face into his chest. He looked around to see where the sound came from, but in the dimly lit crowded parking lot, he wasn't able to make out just what the sound was, or where it had come from. He went to reach for his gun, but felt an empty space at the small of his back. He had forgotten that he left the gun in his car because he was going to the concert.

"Let's get the fuck outta here." Jones grabbed hold of Farren's hand, practically dragging her across the parking lot toward his car.

"As much as I want to go, we have to call the police! I can't just leave!" She was almost hysterical, and he didn't want to do anything but reassure her that everything was going to be alright.

Jones ran his hand down his face. He hated being out in the open without knowing what or who was out there lurking. "Fine, we'll call the police from my car."

I hate the fucking cops! His mind protested as soon as the words left his mouth. Ever since he was old enough to understand what his family truly did for a living, he didn't trust a cop, and especially after a dirty cop had kidnapped his best friend's girl.

Once they were safely inside his vehicle, he dialed 911, and they waited for the police to arrive. Farren was still shaking, and he wanted to hold her desperately. But as much as he knew about her, she knew little to nothing about him.

It took the Dallas Metro Police Department over an hour to arrive. Since it was a well-known fact that the D.M.P.D. was extremely short-handed, Jones wasn't at all surprised. The two patrol officers seemed to be irritated by the fact that they had to do their jobs as they were taking Farren's statement, and it took everything in Jones not to punch the arrogant assholes in the throat.

"Should you even be questioning her out in the open like this? What if the guy who did it is still out there?" Jones was tired of these assholes, and they were putting Farren's safety in jeopardy.

"First of all, we aren't even sure of what Ms. Bell witnessed if anything, so you need to calm down, sir," the officer snidely replied.

Jones took a step forward, but Farren grabbed his hand and gave him a small, reassuring smile. He was supposed to be comforting her, but he almost let his temper get the best of him, and now she was the one calming him down.

Jones nodded his head, letting her know he would back off, but the asshole was on thin ice. The smart-ass cop and his partner finished questioning Farren without pissing him off any further, but he was still leery of their detective skills.

The two officers went off in the direction Farren told them the crime happened, and not long after, there was plenty of commotion confirming exactly what Farren saw. It didn't take long for the cavalry to arrive. The county coroner, ambulance, and more police officers swarmed the scene.

The concert was still in full swing, but with all of the fuss going on, it was causing a crowd to gather. Jones didn't want or need for anyone to see Farren talking to the cops, so he thought it was a good idea for them to leave.

Jones found the detective that was put in charge of the investigation and handed him his card. "Detective Carson, if you need to ask Ms. Bell any more questions, you can call me."

Farren stayed quiet, but her eyes widened a little. Jones had no idea what she was thinking, but he couldn't let her stay out in the open like this. It was too dangerous.

The detective narrowed his eyes at Jones. "Who are you, her lawyer or something?"

"Doesn't matter who I am. We're leaving. If you need anything, give me a call."

"She's a witness. You can't just leave." The detective's brow was creased, and his smooth brown face had instantly filled with anger.

"You've got her statement. She's been through enough, and you guys haven't even taken into consideration that the person who did this could be watching everything. He could very well know that Farren is a witness." Jones growled out the statement through clenched teeth.

The detective seemed reluctant to let them go, but Jones knew that it was best if Farren left the scene, and the cop knew that too.

"Fine, but make sure you are available for further questioning." The detective glared at Farren.

"Why are you treating me like a suspect? I'm the one who called you all. I won't be going anywhere, I live and work here. But I tell you what, you can contact Mr. Sullivan and my attorney if you have any further questions," Farren replied before flouncing away toward Jones' SUV.

Jones couldn't help but smile at the sassy retort. That was the woman he had come to know, fierce and unapologetic. He was glad to see that even through a traumatic experience, her personality shined.

————

Both Jones and Farren agreed that she was in no condition to drive, so he had Jasper go and pick up their brother, Jax to drive Farren's car. After they got the car situated, Jones left the parking lot like a bat out of hell. He wanted to get far away from this mess, but he knew no matter how fast he drove, this was only the beginning.

Jones headed toward his downtown apartment because it was only ten minutes away. He spared a glance in Farren's direction, and she was gazing out the window with tears still silently streaming down her heart-shaped face. She had remained strong while talking to the police, but he wasn't surprised that the night had finally taken its toll. It broke his heart to see her so broken and afraid. It was like his hand had a mind of its own when he reached across the console and grabbed her hand to hold it.

She gave him a watery smile and squeezed his hand in acknowledgment, but she didn't let it go. He didn't want to contemplate why his heart began to race at that simple gesture, so he returned his attention back to the road.

CHAPTER FIVE

FARREN

Farren let her gaze stay outside of the window. No matter how hard she tried to forget what she witnessed, she just couldn't shake the vision of the man dying right in front of her. She was able to keep her composure while talking to the police, but now that it was all said and done, she couldn't keep the tears at bay.

Farren never would've been able to get through the night without Jones' help. She never would've guessed him to be so compassionate. Farren always thought of him as aloof or uncaring. Although they had never interacted one on one, she had to admit that her impression of him was completely wrong.

Jones had not only stayed with her, but he'd done everything in his power to comfort, protect, and even stand up for her without being asked. Farren wasn't the type of woman that needed to be saved. As a matter of fact, she could always handle things on her own. However, it was nice not having to do that tonight. She appreciated the fact that Jones came in and took charge without being overbearing. He took care of her when she needed it most, and for that, she would be eternally grateful.

Farren finally shook herself out of the haze she had been in when Jones pulled up to a posh downtown apartment building. She couldn't help but admire the opulence of the place, and they were only in the valet.

"Uh, so I guess you're not taking me home?" she questioned, biting her bottom lip. Farren didn't know why she felt shy all of a sudden. She decided just to let him handle the cops because her mind and emotions were all over the place, but taking her to his apartment was a step beyond what she was expecting.

"No. I don't think it's wise that you go home right now. If you want, you can call Eden and she can come over, but I don't think it's smart for you to go anywhere unprotected."

Farren didn't want to get her best friend mixed up in whatever nonsense situation that she stumbled upon, so she would go with Jones and call Eden later.

"You're right. I don't want to be alone anyway. So, I guess you have a house guest for now." When Jones gave her a wicked smile, she couldn't help the shiver that ran down her spine.

Even though Jones wasn't exactly her type, she could admit that he was one fine specimen. His hazel eyes gleamed with flecks of gold and always held a hint of danger in them. She couldn't help but look away from his intense gaze, but her eyes seemed to have a mind of their own as they roamed over the reddish tan of his skin that seemed to glow with every delicious move of his sculpted body. As he exited the car, Farren watched every one of his muscles flex as he smoothly rounded the vehicle to open her door. She shook her head to get herself together as he led her into the swanky building.

Farren gave a little whistle as Jones held her hand through the opulent lobby. She couldn't imagine living in a place this fancy. Her apartment, while extremely nice, had nothing on this place. Once they reached the elevator, she thought that Jones would let her hand go... but he didn't.

Farren didn't have it in her to fight against the strange connection she felt with this man. She just chalked it up to her distress and decided a good night's sleep was what she needed to get her mind right.

When they arrived at his apartment, again she was impressed. The view of Victory Park through the floor to ceiling windows was immaculate. She instantly dropped her purse and walked toward the windows. The lights twinkled and winked at her in the distance; the hustle and bustle of the late night partiers couldn't be heard, but she could feel the energy like it had its own heartbeat.

"Wow! You've got some view." The awe in Farren's voice couldn't be denied.

"Indeed, I most certainly do." The seductive tone in Jones' voice gave Farren the chills.

She looked over her shoulder to chastise him for being arrogant, but the words were caught in her throat when she realized he was looking directly at her. Farren could feel the blush creep up her face, and she couldn't tear her eyes away from his.

His hazel eyes glinted with a passion that Farren couldn't believe was directed at her. She finally tore her eyes away, shaking her head to try to disconnect the electricity between them, then turned around and directed her attention toward the view once more.

"It really is a wonderful view you have," Farren whispered, trying to break the sexual tension.

Farren didn't hear when Jones moved, but she could feel his presence getting closer to her. She felt the heat from his body close to her back, and she was afraid of what she would do if she turned around.

She felt his strong hands on her shoulders as he turned her slowly to face him. Her eyes flicked up quickly to his strong jaw covered in a five o'clock shadow, over his slightly crooked nose and his round bright eyes. He was gorgeous in a way that Farren couldn't help but notice. She could see the concern reflected in his eyes, but the passion she saw made her reassess her thoughts about Jones Sullivan.

Farren's head tilted to the side in assessment of the man that was now a total enigma. When her eyes finished their roaming, she noticed that his perfectly shaped lips had ticked up slightly at the corners in a devilishly sexy smirk. She couldn't help the shy smile that graced her plump lips.

Before she could blink, he leaned over and firmly pressed his mouth against hers. His lips held just the right amount of softness, and Farren found herself moaning and pressing her breasts up against his firm chest. Their lips locked in a passionate kiss that came out of nowhere, but she'd be damned if she complained. After everything that happened tonight, she welcomed the distraction. The last thing she wanted to think about was seeing someone lose their life.

His insistent tongue prodded her lips to open, and she willingly obeyed his silent demand opening her mouth to give him access. Their tongues swirled around each other, Farren reveling in his taste. She could feel her body starting to respond. The heat crept up in a slow simmer, and the longer she stayed pressed up against this beast of a man, she could feel his hunger radiating through him.

Farren could hear herself moaning louder, pressing herself against him harder, and she couldn't stop her hips from rotating against the large bulge in his pants. She felt wanton, starved for this man that she barely knew, but she didn't care.

Suddenly, Jones slowed the kiss and nibbled on her lips. Farren whimpered in protest, but she knew he did the right thing when he pulled back from her. Although he didn't say a word, the message in his eyes was loud and clear. *They were not finished!*

"You've been through a lot tonight." It was a statement of fact, so Farren didn't respond. "You should get some rest." Jones' deep voice rumbled as his eyes roamed freely across her face.

Farren swallowed hard at the look he was giving her, but there was no moisture, *in her throat at least*, so she nodded her head in response. Jones slowly walked to the other side of the large living room and flipped off the lights as she silently followed behind him as he led her down a long hallway into a room.

The setup of his guest room was spectacular. The room was bathed in a soft light that made the entire room glow in a warm gold. The large queen bed looked like a dream with some of the biggest, softest looking pillows Farren had ever seen. *Or maybe I'm just tired*, she thought as she absently ran her hand over the plush comforter. This night was one for the record books for sure.

———

After Jones led her to her temporary quarters, Farren sat deep in thought replaying the night's events. She still couldn't wrap her brain around everything that happened, and most of all, she hoped the murderer hadn't stuck around to see her talking to the police.

When Jones entered the room to check on her, Farren couldn't help but ask the question that was rattling around her brain. "Do you think I'm in danger?"

Her growing concerns were starting to eat at her, and she could no longer hide her fear.

"I think it's a good possibility."

Farren turned to stare wide-eyed at Jones. *Well damn*, Farren thought as she pursed her lips.

"I want to be truthful with you, Farren. This is an unusual situation you're in," Jones stated matter-of-factly.

Farren sighed loudly. "I guess I just wanted it not to be true. You could've lied a little."

"I understand, but I'm not really the sugarcoating type." Jones gave her a small smile.

Farren was exhausted, and before she could stop herself, she yawned loudly. "Excuse me, sorry about that." She smiled sheepishly. "I'm tired. I should really try to get some rest."

Jones nodded, but paused before replying, "Goodnight, Farren."

"Thanks for everything, Jones. I... I don't know what I would've done if you weren't there." Farren gave Jones a tired smile.

"There's no need to thank me..." Jones trailed off, and Farren had a feeling that he wanted to say more, but he just nodded again before he turned and walked out of the room.

Farren knew that she would eventually analyze all the events from tonight, including the mind-blowing kiss she and Jones shared, but right now she would do her best to get some rest so that she could face the unimaginable consequences of the situation she found herself in.

Right as Farren felt herself dozing off, she heard her cell phone buzz in her purse. She cringed when she saw the caller id. With all of the tension of the night, she totally forgot about calling Eden.

"Hey E, what's up?" Farren tried to sound casual, but even she could hear the stress in her voice.

"Don't what's up me, Farren Nicole Bell!"

"Damn, you didn't have to use my entire government name, Eden." Farren sighed. Eden was the mother hen of her group of friends, so she knew that she was about to get slammed with a million questions.

"Farren, I can't believe you didn't call me after what happened tonight. You know I almost had a heart attack when I heard about what went down at the concert."

Farren could hear the wobble in Eden's voice, and she instantly felt like crap. Her best friend had been through so much. Eden was practically stalked by her ex-boyfriend, kidnapped by a dirty cop, and shot at by criminals. After all of that, Eden seemed to become even more concerned about her friends, mothering them to death, not that Farren could blame her.

"I'm sorry. I just didn't want to drop all of this on you until I got my head clear. I didn't mean to worry you, E."

Eden sighed, but Farren knew she was going to give in without any further argument. "I know you didn't mean to worry me, but you did. I saw on the news that somebody was killed..."

Farren's breath hitched. *Oh shit! Were there news cameras there? I can't remember. Was I on the news! Damn it, this cannot be happening.* Farren's thoughts were racing, but she didn't want to scare Eden any more than she already was, so she took a deep breath to calm down.

"E, was I on the news? Di-did you see me on the news?" Farren questioned slowly, but she couldn't keep the worry from seeping into her words.

"No, I didn't see you on the news. Why would I see you on the news?" Farren could hear the confusion in Eden's voice, but she was so relieved that her face wasn't plastered all over the TV for the world to see, she didn't even address Eden's question.

"Did Jones call you guys?"

"About the news? No, why would Jones call?" Eden questioned slowly. "I saw on TV that there was a possible homicide outside of the venue where the concert was held, and I tried to call you, but you didn't answer or call me back."

"I'm sorry. It's been a long night..." Farren trailed off. "A lot has happened tonight, and I promise to tell you everything tomorrow, but right now I need to lay down and rest because I just can't think about this shit anymore." Her voice cracked on the last word. She just wanted to close her eyes without replaying the gruesome scene. Farren wished she could just forget the night had ever happened.

"Okay. I know something is going on with you, but I can hear it in your voice that you don't want to talk about it. Just promise me you'll call first thing tomorrow," Eden responded, her words laced with trepidation.

"I promise. And E, I'm fine. Please don't worry, okay?"

"Okay."

"I'll call you tomorrow. Bye bestie." Farren disconnected the call before Eden had a chance to say anything else. She could feel herself starting to break, and that was the last thing she needed.

Farren lay back on the cloud-soft pillows and drifted off into a restless sleep.

CHAPTER SIX

JONES

Jones sat in the dark sipping his favorite whiskey. He couldn't believe how his night had turned out. He got way more than he bargained for when he agreed to go to that concert. While he sat daydreaming about Farren, she was watching a man die.

Jones shook his head. How in the hell did she find herself in a back alley anyway? The thought of her getting hurt was something he couldn't fathom. He took another sip of the dark liquid and let the burn resonate in his chest. He had to do everything he could to help Farren.

The beeping of his cell gained his attention. It was officer Michaels returning his message from earlier. Linda Michaels was an old friend of Jones' family. She practically grew up with the Sullivan bunch, following his older brother James around like a lovesick puppy. For a long time, she was the only female in their house besides their mother.

Linda was a good friend, and the best insider of the police department that Jones could ask for. Jones read the text message then reread it again. It had to be some mistake, but Linda Michaels didn't make mistakes.

Linda: Peter Ryan.

Jones: Fuck. The mayor's nephew?
Linda: One in the same.
Jones: Info
Linda: I'll call you later with the details
Jones: Thx

Jones suspected that when Linda called it would be an interesting conversation. If the mayor's nephew was the person Farren saw murdered tonight, and with the way the police handled the scene, it was bound to be a whole world of trouble come their way.

Jones decided to check in on Farren once more before he went to his bedroom to wait for Linda's call. He opened the door slowly. It was his intention just to peek his head into the room to see if she was asleep, but when he caught a glimpse of her sleeping form he couldn't help but to quietly slip into the room. He felt like a real creep, but he couldn't help himself.

Farren was laying snuggled under the blankets with just her head barely sticking out. She looked like a little girl curled tightly into a ball. She looked so innocent, even with the small frown she wore in her sleep. Jones wanted to kiss her lips until she smiled. He had the urge to hold her and make sure she understood that he would never let anything happen to her.

Farren whimpered, kicked the blanket off, and turned over as if she were having a bad dream. Jones decided that standing over her in the middle of the night was a certified stalker move, so he tucked her back under the blanket, rubbed her cheek to sooth her, and silently left the room.

Jones wished that they knew each other well enough for him to hold her in his arms in comfort. He wanted to do more than just stand by helplessly. If it was the last thing he did, he would make sure Farren was safe, so he could hold her exactly the way he wanted.

FARREN

Farren thought she felt someone looking at her, but when she turned over, she was in the room alone. The events of the night had caught up to her, and no matter how tired she felt, she couldn't stay asleep.

Every time she closed her eyes, she saw knives and blood. A shiver ran down her spine and she snuggled under the soft blanket and closed her eyes once more.

If she could just get through tonight, maybe she could think of a way to get past all of this. Farren wasn't big on therapy, but she decided that she would definitely need to talk to someone about what she saw. It wasn't every day you saw someone's life snuffed out in an alley.

Farren lay in the bed looking at the ceiling for what seemed like hours. Her thoughts were all over the place, but she made a conscious effort to keep her mind off the murder.

She decided to think about why she allowed Jones to kiss the hell out of her, and why she liked it so much. The feel of his lips pressed against her were causing a stir deep in her lower belly. He wasn't at all hesitant to take what he wanted, and that was sexy as hell.

She and Jones had limited interactions with one another. Every time they saw each other, it was with a group of friends. They always exchanged pleasantries, but they never really had an in depth conversation. She couldn't even remember if they ever even interacted one on one. So Farren really couldn't figure out what drove Jones to kiss her.

Farren was well aware of Jones' penchant for the ladies. She had seen him talk to a new woman every time they were out. However, she had to admit that even though he would always talk to women, he never left with anybody. And she had never seen him on a date. Farren really only heard rumors about Jones' sexual escapades, she'd never seen it for herself. In fact, even when she was at Euphoria, she never saw Jones. And according to Eden, that was his favorite place to play.

The way Jones helped her, the comfort he offered, hell even the place to lay her head was so beyond what just an acquaintance would do. He literally held her hand through the entire fiasco, and who could forget about the kiss he gave her. All of those things were more than what even a friend would be expected to do.

Jones didn't seem like the type of man that would take advantage of a woman while she was vulnerable. And Farren was positive that wasn't the case in this instance, either. However, she still couldn't come up with a reason he would kiss her.

Farren finally began to doze off, the thoughts of Jones and the kiss they shared still dancing around her brain. She couldn't help but wonder what if they hadn't stopped kissing, what if they'd fallen into each other, and she'd lost herself in him the way she wanted to do.

What if I lost myself with Jones?

MURDERER

"You told me to take care of the problem. The problem is taken care of," the murderer with pale blue eyes stated matter-of-factly.

"I told you to take care of Peter. Now, according to my sources at Dallas Metro, there are witness to what happened. What the fuck were you thinking?!"

"I swear Dallas Metro is a fucking joke." The man sighed. "Look, I know what I'm doing, the opportunity was there. He was alone for once. The entourage he always has around was inside the concert. I did what needed to be done."

"It could've been cleaner. If someone can identify you, we're both up shit creek."

"Relax, we've known each other twenty years. You know I'm a ghost, and if anybody can see spirits, they'll become one."

Chapter Seven

JONES

"*As the chief stated already, it is early in the investigation, so we are still looking at possible motives. At this point, mugging is also being considered.*"

Jones flicked the TV off. "What a load of horseshit!" he mumbled, stalking toward his kitchen. Last night was long and tedious. He stayed up half the night contacting his connections to find out exactly what the police knew about what Farren saw. One thing was for certain, that was no mugging she'd witnessed in that alley.

After Linda called, he found out the police didn't have a clue as to who killed Peter Ryan. There wasn't any evidence to suggest that the murder was a mugging, especially since Peter still had on all his jewelry. Linda also revealed that the list of witnesses to the crime was short, and Farren's name was on it.

Jones knew of the victim, Peter Ryan because anybody with connections to the criminal world knew exactly who he was. The guy was a scumbag, to say the least, and he could've been killed for any number of reasons. But mugging... definitely not.

As Jones began pouring a cup of coffee, he heard when Farren entered the kitchen. He was glad he had been distracted the night before. Looking for a killer kept his mind off the beautiful woman that was sleeping in his guest room. And after he tasted those luscious lips of hers, he was proud of himself for not going in there, crawling into bed with her, and making them both forget all their worries.

It had been a dream of his since he first laid eyes on her to have her in his bed. The thought of her being so close and not being able to touch her was a form of pure torture.

"Good morning." Farren's voice was low and sexy, husky from sleep and it made Jones instantly harden at the sound.

He turned and greeted her with a broad smile. Her hair was all over her head, and it seemed she had found a pair of his shorts and a t-shirt that looked much better on her than they ever did on him.

"Mornin'. How'd you sleep?" Jones sipped his coffee, his eyes never leaving the tantalizing view that Farren presented. The t-shirt was very big on her, but it still didn't hide the curves of her succulent breasts.

"I don't think what I did could be categorized as sleeping." She sighed and gave him a small, sad smile. "But it's not because of that magnificent heaven you call a guest room."

Jones smiled. "I'm glad you liked it. Want some coffee? Because we need to talk."

He didn't wait for her to reply as he turned and retrieved her a mug. He sat the coffee in front of her, and she sighed as she approached the counter.

"Nobody ever wants to hear, 'we need to talk' before coffee." Farren sat down and sipped the hot beverage with a small moan. "Okay, lay it on me."

"You're not safe." Jones just gave it to her straight. He wasn't the type of man to beat around the bush.

Farren nodded her response, but Jones noticed her eyes seem to glaze over slightly. Jones didn't want to frighten her, but it was more dangerous for her to be in the dark about what was going on.

"The guy you saw murdered last night was the mayor's nephew." The lack of recognition on her face told him she had no idea who he was talking about. "His name was Peter Ryan."

"Shit. That guy is nothing but trouble."

Jones' face creased in confusion. *What the hell did she know about Peter Ryan?* "Are you familiar with the guy?"

"I didn't know him personally if that's what you're asking." She shook her head and shrugged. "Look, I see all kinds of seedy shit working at the radio station, especially during the concerts. I didn't know he was related to the mayor even with the same surname. But the name Peter Ryan is synonymous with dealer... well, at least it was anyways. I can't believe he was the guy I saw killed. Shit, I can't believe he was the mayor's damn nephew. Talk about black sheep."

"You have no idea. So, you didn't recognize Peter, but did you recognize the guy he was fighting? I know last night you said you didn't but now since everything has calmed down, do you remember ever seeing him?"

"I thought about it all last night, but no, I don't recall ever seeing him before. It was dark in the alley, but when he passed me, I saw his face as clear as I'm looking at yours right now. I'll never forget what he looked like, especially his eyes. They were distinctive, unforgettable even. I've never seen anyone else with eyes like that." She rubbed her arms in an up and down motion like she was fighting away a chill.

"They were this pale blue color, and so cold they made me shiver. Even with the short glimpse of him, I knew that wasn't his first time taking a life." Jones watched as she shook again and pushed the mug away from her. He could tell that last night's events were weighing heavily on her.

"So why do you think I'm in danger?" she finally asked, looking at him wearily.

"There was a press conference this morning. The police released a possible motive as a mugging. My contacts told me that Ryan still had all of his expensive jewelry. Which means they don't have any fuckin' clue as to who did this or why." He took a deep breath not really wanting to tell her about the witness list, but he had to.

Farren nodded. "But nobody knows that I saw anything except for that detective."

"Dallas Metro has so many leaks that its nickname is the Titanic, and I know for a fact that your name is on a witness list."

Farren's eyes went wide with fear, but he continued on because she deserved to know the truth.

"I don't trust those bumbling idiots not to have that witness list, and even your address and statement just lying around somewhere. I know more about this case than that asshole detective, and that's a problem."

"Well shit." Farren huffed. "I appreciate your hospitality and all, but I can't just stay here while the Titanic sinks. What if this lunatic comes after me? What the hell am I supposed to do?" Jones could see the rising hysteria in her honey-colored eyes before she put her head down on the counter in defeat. He couldn't blame her, but the last thing she needed was to lose it.

Jones walked around the counter and rubbed her back in a soothing gesture. He was no good at this emotional shit. He'd grown up with six brothers and was practically grown when his little sister finally came along.

He lifted her chin and softly kissed her lips hoping to calm her. However, the kiss did nothing to calm him. She looked up at him with her eyes red-rimmed and watery.

It pissed him off that she was so scared, but he did his best to calm her. "Listen, nothing will happen to you, Farren. I promise."

"How can you promise me something like that?" She sniffled, her face full of curiosity, but at least Jones didn't see the outright denial of what he was saying.

"Because I'm me." He gave her his most charming smile hoping against hope that she would believe him. "And I don't make promises I don't intend to keep."

Farren gave him a genuine smile. "Well, for my sake I hope that's the truth."

———

After their talk, Farren excused herself back to the guest room. Jones knew that he couldn't keep her locked up in his place like some princess in an ivory tower, but the thought of her being in danger made him want to do exactly that. However, he knew that he had to get to the bottom of what was going on so Farren could get back to her life. *And away from me.* He shook his head to dispel the negative thoughts. This wasn't about him.

He had hit up all his contacts the night before, and he was waiting on a few to get back to him. So, he decided that he should finally call his best friend, Camedon, and let him know what was going on.

"Hey, Sullivan. What's up?" Camedon's voice came through clear after one ring.

"A lot, actually."

"Yeah? What's going on, man? I don't think I've ever heard you sound so... stressed."

"Stressed is an understatement. Look, can you drop by my place? There's too much going on to explain over the phone." Jones took a deep breath as he ran his hand through his hair.

"Alright, sure man. I can be there in thirty."

"Great. Oh, and Cam... bring Eden."

"Uh, yeah okay," Camedon hesitantly replied.

Thirty-five minutes later, there was a knock on the door. Jones opened it to a serious faced Camedon and a gorgeous, smiling Eden. "Hey guys, come on in."

"Hey, Jones," Eden greeted brightly as she gave him a side hug and a kiss on the cheek. Camedon nodded, and they gave each other the custom, one-armed man hug before he followed Eden into the living room.

Jones had already told Farren that he invited their best friends over, so they could let them know what was going on. She didn't freak out, but she commented that she wasn't thrilled at the prospect of answering all of Eden's questions either.

"You guys want a drink?"

"No, we're good. So, what's this about?" Camedon questioned, getting straight to the point.

"It's about me, Cam." Farren strolled into the room as if she had been living there for years. Jones didn't hate it. He liked how comfortable she looked in his place.

Jones watched as Eden's eyes widened, and she looked at Farren then back at him then back at Farren again. Her mouth was hanging open in disbelief. Camedon sat smirking at them both, and Jones knew instantly that they had the wrong idea. Well, not *completely* wrong.

He held his hands up in a surrendering gesture. "It's not what you think."

"Hey, you all are grown. I don't think anything," Camedon commented, still smirking mischievously.

"Grown my ass. It's before noon! What are you doing here this early? Were you here last night when we talked?" Eden questioned, her eyes getting bigger with each question.

Farren placed her hands on her round hips and cocked her head to the side. "Now, him I can excuse. But you know damn well it isn't like that, E."

Jones didn't know if he should be offended or not, but he decided to keep his comments to himself.

"Then what's it like, Farren?" Eden stood, placing her hands on her hips mimicking Farren.

Farren sighed heavily. "I saw someone murdered last night. Jones was there to help me."

Eden plopped down on the couch with a thud, all of her bravado leaving her in an instant. Her eyes remained wide for a whole different reason now.

"Murder? The murder that was on the news last night! Are you okay? Oh my God! That's why you were freaking out about the news broadcast! Does anybody know that you saw what happened?"

Jones observed Farren as her best friend rapidly fired question after question at her. He had to admit she took it like a champ. He barely noticed the irritation that flashed in her eyes, but it was there.

"Calm down, Angel. Give the woman a chance to explain. Farren, are you alright?" Camedon stepped in trying to ease his girlfriend's hysterics.

"I will be." Farren looked at Jones, and he couldn't read her expression. However, he was pretty sure she just looked to him for comfort. He gave her a smile of reassurance as she sat down and seemed to relax a little.

"So start from the beginning and don't leave anything out." Eden moved to sit by Farren and took hold of her hand.

Farren went through all the events of the night before. Jones could see the shadow of fear take over her face as she recounted her story. With every word that fell from her beautiful lips, the more he could see the terror etched on her face, and it made him angrier than he thought was possible.

What the hell was going on in that alley? Who was the guy fighting with Peter, and why would he take a chance on killing someone in such a populated area? There was a piece of shit walking around with absolutely no heart. *How could anybody be so uncouth, so uncivilized that they could slit a man's throat with hundreds of people only a few yards away?* None of it made sense. Jones' thoughts were scattered, and he shook his head to focus on the conversation again.

Once Farren was finished with her story, he could still see the slight tremble in her hands. She was making a valiant effort to be strong, and he admired her for that, but he still had to fight the urge to remove Eden's hand and replace it with his own.

"So what now? There are still concerts going on. Are you working tonight?" Eden asked, her face filled with worry.

Farren ran her fingers through her hair. "No, I don't work tonight. I have a few days off. I don't work again until Sunday. But I can call in. Besides, nobody at work knows that I witnessed what happened."

"Don't worry about calling in. The concerts have been postponed until further notice."

Farren's face scrunched up, her eyes narrowed at Jones before she pursed her lips. "How do you know the concerts have been postponed? I haven't gotten so much as a text from the station."

"You will. I told you, I have connections everywhere. Plus, I promised." He winked at her, and he could've sworn she melted just a little.

Chapter Eight

FARREN

Farren didn't know how he knew it, but Jones was right. The concerts were postponed for a later date. The station general manager called a meeting where he proceeded to tell the staff that the loss of the mayor's nephew outside their event could be seen as negative. To stay in the mayor's good graces, the powers that be decided not only to move venues, but also reschedule the event entirely. The station would be cooperating with the investigation anyway that they could to stay in good favor with the police as well as the mayor.

Farren really didn't mind. The thought of going back there gave her anxiety like she'd never felt before. She didn't think she would ever be able to go back to that place again.

It had been two weeks since the murder, and everyone else was going on with life. Meanwhile, she was having night terrors and anxiety attacks at every turn. She'd only gone back to her apartment to get some necessities so that she could stay at Eden's. Everyone insisted that she not be alone right now, and she agreed because she still wasn't comfortable by herself.

When she arrived at her apartment, something felt off. Her doors were still locked when she arrived, but she couldn't dismiss the feeling that someone had been in her apartment. She meticulously went through her home, but nothing was out of place. Farren chalked it up to her being hypersensitive after what happened.

When she told her friends about the funny feeling she had, Jones suggested that she continue staying with him, but she didn't think that was necessary. She could easily just stay at Eden's. But Farren had to admit that Jones' offer made her think. It also made her uncomfortable in the juiciest of ways, and after that scorching hot kiss, she couldn't trust herself around him.

His hazel eyes seemed to see right to her inner naughtiness, and she couldn't help but feel like she was naked whenever he looked at her, no matter what she was wearing. He was definitely an interesting guy, and one good thing that came out of this whole ordeal was that Farren got to see another side to Jones Sullivan.

She knew that he was sexy because anyone with eyes could see that. But she didn't know just how sexy he was. He had a calm demeanor but a take charge attitude. Jones was a man that knew what he wanted and got it. Although he was clearly successful, he didn't flaunt his wealth, and he wasn't boastful. However, the way he carried himself, you knew what type of man he was.

But, underneath all that charismatic sexiness, Farren saw the danger lurking. The way he handled that detective when he threatened her. The cool, collected guy he had been all night held a fire in his eyes like she'd never seen. Farren couldn't say that she was more than a little turned on by it.

She found herself in a precarious situation; she was attracted to this man like she'd never been attracted to anyone before. And although they ran in the same circle because of their best friends dating, the thought of dating and especially having sex with Jones never crossed her mind.

Farren was a red-blooded woman, and she could appreciate an attractive man when she saw one no matter his race or ethnicity, but she never thought she would be sexually attracted to a white man. She and her friends had had many conversations about interracial dating since her bestie started seriously dating a white man, but Farren never thought that she would be interested in dating a white guy. But she had to admit there was something about Jones that she just couldn't dismiss.

Farren knew that her emotions were all over the place, and she could definitely blame her increased feelings for Jones on temporary insanity, but she wasn't the type of girl that lied to herself.

She was the kind of woman that faced things head on—every challenge, every choice, every consequence. She didn't back down. But for the first time in her life, she was scared. The situation she was in was perilous. If anyone recognized or saw her that night, she could put not only herself but her loved ones in danger, and she didn't want that to happen.

So as attracted to Jones as she was, starting up something new was not something she could afford to do at the moment. The only reason she agreed to stay at Eden's place was that with her living with Camedon now, they had more than enough room. They also had security everywhere. After what happened to Eden, she still had a bodyguard who drove her to and from work, so Farren knew she wouldn't be putting her in danger. And being the overprotective friend that she was, Eden insisted that Farren had her own protection, at least until she heard back from the detectives.

Farren argued that she didn't need a bodyguard and that would draw more attention to her, but Eden wouldn't let up on her nagging. After two weeks with no threats or anything else that could be considered unusual, Farren didn't think anybody knew about what she saw, so she felt like she didn't need a bodyguard. But both Jones and Camedon vetoed that thought before it even left her mind, so Farren relented and agreed to let someone drive her around for the time being.

It wasn't a big deal in the end because the bodyguards were so quiet, she forgot that they were there most of the time. As a matter of fact, there were some questioning stares from her co-workers when she showed up to the emergency meeting that was called with Benny in tow. He was quiet, but his imposing figure stood well over six feet. His lean body was muscular, and his face held a "don't mess with me" expression at all times. His almost coal black eyes made him look menacing, but Farren knew that underneath all that he was a genuinely nice man.

At the mention of her meeting, Camedon suggested Benny tag along with her. When she went to protest, Jones insisted that he not just drive her, but accompany her into the building. The way he took charge made the protest die on her lips. She wasn't some weak woman that melted at the thought of a bossy man, but with Jones, she felt almost compelled to do what he asked, or demanded.

"We're here, Ms. Farren." Benny's deep voice rang from the front seat.

Benny pulled up to the front of Eden's building before Farren even realized the car was moving. She was so deep in thought that the ride from the station had zoomed by quickly.

"Oh. Right. Uh, Benny, you know you can just call me Farren. We're probably the same age. I feel like Ms. Daisy or something."

Benny let out a chuckle. "Just a habit of the job, ma'am. No offense meant. Just a bit of professionalism."

Farren could understand that. "Well alright, Mr. Benny. We can keep it professional until we know each other a little better. We'll have nicknames before you know it." Farren winked at him before sliding out of the car. She heard his laughter as she shut the door behind her.

———

Farren pushed the code into the elevator for the penthouse apartment. She still couldn't get over the luxury of it all. The situation wasn't ideal, but she couldn't help but to enjoy her surroundings. She was happy that Eden had a chance to live the highlife, and she was so glad that her best friend found a person to love her as much as Camedon did. She had been so worried that Eden would marry her loser ex-boyfriend Bo, but she'd claimed to be happy. So Farren had to sit and watch Eden pretend to be satisfied with a dirtbag. She was so glad when Eden found out he was cheating and left his ass without a second thought.

Now if only she could get her own life together, Farren might have a chance at her own love and happiness. *I can only hope.*

Farren walked into the penthouse to the sound of deep voices. It wasn't early, but she wasn't expecting anyone to be back so soon. She knew that Eden was in meetings for most of the day, and she thought that Camedon had to check on a property on the other side of town.

She continued cautiously in the direction of the voices. Farren laughed at herself for being so scary. There was no way on God's green earth that anyone could get into this place without permission, so she smiled and relaxed. When she got to the living area, she was surprised to see Harper, Camedon's younger brother, and Jones talking and laughing liked they lived there.

I guess that's how they do things around here. Just post up in each other's houses.

Farren hadn't completely entered the room when Harper graced her with a dazzling smile. Harper was a certified mess, but he was fun and goofy, and his personality was exactly what she needed.

"Well well, if it isn't Cola. I could never mistake that Coke bottle shape." Harper winked as he walked toward her with his massive arms opened wide.

Farren thought she heard a growl but dismissed it. She laughed and walked directly into his arms. She felt comfort in his warm, brotherly embrace. "If I didn't think of you as my brother, I might believe that you were flirting with me Mr. Price."

"You know I can't help but flirt when a woman as beautiful as you walks into the room. Even if she does treat me like her brother." He kissed the top of her head warmly, and she smiled against his chest.

She heard another growl, and this time it was no mistake. The sound was loud and clear. Farren stepped back and her eyes locked onto an angry pair that was glaring at Harper in a way that surprised her.

"Jones, are you okay?" Farren questioned as she stepped further away from Harper and closer to Jones. His fists were held tightly at his sides, but he kept staring at Harper.

Farren looked at Harper to try and gauge the situation, and he was smirking with that ever present mischievous glint in his blue-gray eyes.

"Jones?" Farren didn't know what was going on. *Maybe they were arguing before I got here*, she thought as she continued to try to get Jones' attention.

"Oh, he's okay, Cola, or I think I'll just call you CB for Coke bottle

..." Harper rambled on behind her like he wasn't getting the death glare from his friend.

"I'm fine, sweetheart. How'd the meeting go?" Jones looked at her expectantly like he wasn't just standing there growling at his best friend's brother.

Farren shook her head. *Crazy ass men. If he wants to pretend he wasn't just growling, so can I.* "Uh, the meeting was okay. What are you two doing here? Anything happen that I need to know about?"

"No, there haven't been any new developments. My contact told me they still have no idea who killed Peter, so I expect them to come knocking for another interview with you soon."

Farren expected as much. The murder was *the* hot story, and it was on nearly every news station in the state of Texas. The police were under a lot of pressure to close the case even though it had only been a couple of weeks.

"I figured as much, but I thought they would do a follow-up quicker."

"It will be fine. When they want to talk, they can come here, where you're safe, and with a lawyer." Farren could tell Jones was not going to budge so she didn't argue with him.

She agreed that she should have a lawyer present after the way that detective spoke to her the first time. Farren didn't like the snide remarks or the lightly veiled threats.

"So what are you guys doing here?" Farren asked again. She noticed that neither of them had answered her before.

"Well, I'm doing my monthly drop-in." Harper shrugged. Farren knew that there was more to Harper's visit than what he let on, but she wouldn't call him on it.

Since she met Harper, he had been chasing after Eden's twin sister, Elyse. They had been playing this cat and mouse game for months but to each their own. Maybe it was some kind of foreplay for them. Hell, Farren couldn't judge.

"Uh huh. Well, it's good to see you, Harp." She winked, and he blushed, giving away that he knew he wasn't fooling her.

"And you? What are you doing here sir?" Farren could've sworn Jones' eyes turned a darker shade at her words, but she refused to acknowledge it. She knew what type of lifestyle Jones led. Club Euphoria was the home for all kinds of freakiness, but she wasn't aware that Jones was into the Dom thing. She did know, however, that he was very free with his love, and she couldn't blame him for sharing his magnificent body. Farren was going to stick with her decision to focus on getting herself out of this mess. She didn't think starting something new was the right thing to do, but Jones was a temptation she couldn't seem to resist, especially after the heated kiss they'd shared. Even with the obvious connection they had, Farren had never been with a white man before, and she didn't think Jones would like to be her experiment to see what they were like. Hell, she wouldn't want any man to experiment with her, but Jones wasn't the type of man you had a relationship with. He was the kind of guy you slept with, not introduce to your parents. *Or is he?*

"I'm here for you, Farren." Jones finally answered her question with a predatory smile. The look on his face made her forget the decision she just made. Shit, that look made her forget her own name.

"Wha-what do you mean? You're here for me?" Farren swallowed hard.

I'm in big trouble.

Chapter Nine

JONES

"Wha-what do you mean? You're here for me?" Farren questioned with wide eyes. Jones watched as she visibly swallowed and squirmed.

Jones almost laughed at the shock that registered on her pretty face. He was pretty certain that she didn't notice her own reactions. He made no secret about wanting her. He couldn't stop the lust filled looks that he gave her even if he tried. Jones knew that Farren was an intelligent woman, and she could see his desire, even if she tried to deny it.

"I mean... I came to check up on you. See how you're holding up." He quirked an auburn brow at her in challenge. Jones wanted to see if she would admit what she could clearly see in his eyes... lust.

"Oh. Well um...yeah, I'm holding up alright I guess." Farren looked everywhere but at him, and her cinnamon brown skin was flushed.

Yeah, she sees it, Jones thought with a wicked smile. He couldn't wait to get his hands on her again.

"I thought I would take you out for dinner. You've been stuck here, and only going out for work. I thought you might want a break."

"Oh wow. Yeah, that sounds cool." Farren was still fidgeting. Jones didn't think she was even aware that she was wringing her hands, and blushing.

"Great, I'll give you time to rest a little, and I can come back and pick you up in a couple of hours."

"Cool. But if I'm in danger and can't go home, is it safe to be going out for dinner? Should Benny come with us?"

Jones heard Harper chuckle at her innocent question. With all of his focus on Farren he forgot that Harper was even in the room. Harper knew what kind of man Jones was, and what he was truly capable of. He may not have been in the special forces like Harper, but Jones wasn't always a legitimate business man, and he could definitely handle his own.

Jones narrowed his eyes at Harper before responding to Farren. "No, sweetie. Benny won't be needed because you'll be with me." He gave her a smile that was known to drop a few panties, and he watched as her eyes darkened with lust of their own. *Interesting,* Jones thought as he took in Farren's reaction, his smile growing wider.

"Oh-kay," Farren responded, looking between him and Harper. "So Harper, are you joining us?" Farren smiled brightly at the other man.

Jones knew that he didn't have any reason what so ever to be jealous of Harper, but he was not at all pleased with the idea of Harper's instigating ass on their first date. And that's exactly what this was, their first date, even if Farren was unaware of this fact.

Harper smirked, but Jones kept his face impassive. Jones wouldn't let on just how irritated he actually was.

"Nah, Cola, you guys enjoy yourselves. I have plans for the night." Harper gave Jones a sly wink and a smile. Jones stared at him, his face remaining like stone, but he was going to have a little talk with Harper. Especially about his little nickname for Farren.

"Let me guess... Elyse?" Farren questioned with her own sly smile.

Jones noticed the playfulness leave Harper's eyes for just a split second before the devil may care look was back on his face. *I wonder what that's about?*

"You know me. I always have plans with somebody." Harper's smile was back in place, but it didn't quite meet his eyes before he sauntered from the room.

Jones watched his friend leave the room, and he continued to wonder what was going on with him. He also didn't miss the frown that graced Farren's soft features. Jones himself had never seen Harper behave quite like he just did when he talked about Elyse, so something was definitely up.

Jones shrugged it off. Harper was a grown man, and Jones was not in the habit of getting involved in other people's business, especially if it had to do with relationships. He just wasn't that guy.

Jones slowly approached Farren as she stood still staring after Harper with a frown. He took her small hand in his, gaining her attention. She looked up at him shyly before taking a deep breath and straightening her shoulders.

The shyness disappeared from her in a flash; it was gone so fast he almost thought he imagined it. But he knew it was there. Jones appreciated a confident woman, but the shyness coming from Farren showed a vulnerability that she didn't allow many people to see, and he appreciated that she let him get close enough to witness it.

"So I wanted to take you to Five-Sixty. Ever been there?" Jones questioned getting back on track.

Farren's mouth dropped open in what Jones could only assume was disbelief. It was nearly impossible to get a reservation at the five-star restaurant. People booked months in advance, so it was unbelievable that he could take her there without having prior plans.

"Yes, I've been there once, and it was amazing. I didn't think I would get the opportunity to go back." Farren's eyes, as well as her smile, were bright with excitement.

Jones almost wanted to ask her who had taken her, but he wouldn't show his possessiveness, even if the feeling was something totally new for him. He just wanted to be the first person to introduce her to new things. He wanted to impress her and show her that he was the kind of man that would give her what no other could. Jones still had plans to do just that.

"Well, I'm glad I get to take you back." He gave her a genuine smile as he pulled her into his embrace and kissed the top of her head. "I'll let you get some rest. I'll be back in a couple of hours."

Jones squeezed her gently before he kissed her cheek and left Camedon's apartment. He was excited for the first time in ages. He'd been to the restaurant countless times, but he was happy that he would finally get another opportunity to spend some alone time with Farren.

————

Farren's melodic laugh drifted to his ears once more. She had been so relaxed and laughing all night long. Jones couldn't help the silly comments and stories he had been telling her all evening. He just couldn't get enough of her smile, the amused twinkle in her eyes, and the overall feeling of joy she gave him.

Jones knew that tonight would make a significant shift in their relationship. They would go from being acquaintances to much more. He wanted to know everything about her. Jones thought it would take much more effort to break down her defenses, but he could only guess that the bond they shared from the night of the homicide made things easier.

"Jones, I would never have guessed you were this funny."

Jones smiled at her. "And why wouldn't I be funny?"

Jones watched as she tilted her head to the side, her wispy bangs falling in her face as she smiled at him. "I don't know. You just seem kind of serious all the time. You didn't strike me as the prankster type."

He wanted to reach over and tuck her hair behind her ear, and kiss her so deep that he took her breath away. He settled on moving her hair softly behind her ear. He ran the back of his hand down her cheek in a slow caress. The kiss would come later. Of that he was absolutely positive.

"I grew up with six brothers," he finally answered, shaking himself from the trance she'd unknowingly put him in. "You have to have a sense of humor." He laughed at the look on her face when he mentioned his brothers.

"Let me get this straight... there are seven of you? I thought it was just you and the other two. Your poor mother had seven boys... and from the looks of the you and the other two, I would say seven huge sons," Farren stated with a look of awe on her face.

"No, my mother had eight kids. My sister, Jennifer is the youngest." Jones proudly smiled.

"Well damn! Bless her heart. Did your parents not know..." Farren leaned closer to him and said in a low, conspiratorial whisper, "what birth control was?" she asked with a serious expression, but her eyes danced with mirth.

Jones chuckled. "I'm pretty sure my mom just wanted a girl."

"Well, she's a better woman than me."

"Why is that? Do you not want kids?" Jones asked, frowning. He never thought about having kids before, but hearing Farren possibly not wanting any made him feel some type of way.

"Well, I sure as hell don't want eight." She laughed. "I never really thought about having kids. I didn't grow up with my siblings, so I never had the urge to have a house full of rugrats running around." Farren shrugged her shoulders causing Jones' eyes to caress the bare skin.

His eyes followed the delicate curve of her shoulder down to the luscious outline of her breasts. The dress she wore had tantalized his senses all evening. Jones had to keep telling stories to keep his mind from going to the gutter.

The blush toned dress that made her brown skin glow was by no means tight. It simply hugged her curves in all the right places. It landed right above her knee, but the matching stilettoes that graced her feet made her already long legs look like they went on forever. Jones didn't know how he was going to make it through the night without devouring her, so instead of denying himself the pleasure of touching her, he spent the night brushing her skin with light touches here and there. However, it was beginning not to be enough. He wanted much more.

"Jones? Did I say something wrong?" Farren questioned, bringing Jones back to the present.

"No sweetheart, of course not. It just saddens me that you didn't grow up with a house full of fun like I did. As much as they get on my nerves, I wouldn't trade any of my siblings for the world."

Farren smiled. "Well, like I said, there's no way I would have eight kids. But who knows, maybe one or two might be in my future, if I find the right man... and surrogate." She laughed and winked.

He couldn't help but laugh at her cheekiness. Farren was like no other woman he had ever met. She had this easiness to her that he was drawn to.

The night had gone better than he could've ever expected. Jones got to know more about Farren, and he broke down some of the walls she'd had up. Jones was leading her through the front of the building on the ground floor of the restaurant when Farren suddenly went stock still.

Jones instantly went on high alert. "Baby, what's wrong?"

Farren looked like she had seen a ghost. "That man," Farren whispered not taking her eyes off the door.

Jones looked in the direction that Farren was staring in, and noticed a man standing at the valet. He squinted his eyes because the guy looked vaguely familiar, but he couldn't place his face. The man seemingly noticing Jones' stare looked directly at him. Jones nodded and stepped in front of Farren, blocking her from the man's line of sight. He turned his back and faced Farren who was still visibly shaken up.

"I know that's him. I would never forget his face," she frantically whispered.

"I believe you, sweetheart. I just need you to take a deep breath and calm down for me. He didn't see you, so I need for you not to draw any attention to yourself okay?"

"I can do that, but I can't go out there."

Jones nodded, took her hand, and led her away from the front of the building. There was a bar and lounge they could go into on the same floor. He could also call for reinforcements.

Jones looked back at the valet, and his eyes locked with an eerie pale blue pair. Jones didn't break the stare down, but he did position himself to block Farren from the creepy asshole's view.

The man finally turned away when the valet pulled up in a nondescript SUV, but Jones knew that it wouldn't be the last time he laid eyes on the murdering son of a bitch.

Chapter Ten

FARREN

The night she saw the murderer, Farren couldn't sleep a wink. Her nights were restless, and the murder replayed in her mind every time she closed her eyes for sleep. Nothing had changed in the investigation, and Farren was on edge.

It had been a couple of weeks since she and Jones had seen the guy that murdered Peter Ryan, and she hadn't seen him since that night. She knew that it was most likely a coincidence that she spotted him outside the restaurant, but there was no way in hell she was taking that chance. Benny had been sticking to her like glue while she worked, and she couldn't say that she minded.

Farren was about to leave the station and was packing up to go home when Evan walked into her shared office.

Shit! This guy...

"I need to talk to you about the Solomon Kings interview."

Farren kept back the eye roll she so desperately wanted to let out. There was nothing they needed to talk about. The interview was done and over with. It had been a success and the Solomon Kings raved about her to her boss, Mark. Evan, however, was unprofessional and had disappeared for most of the night. Farren had done all the work, and on top of everything that night... she had seen a man die!

"Okay, what about the interview?" Farren asked cautiously.

"I didn't get a chance to talk to you before you left, but you need to act more professionally when you're in front of bands."

Farren smiled because this had to be a joke. Evan was running around chasing ass, and she was the unprofessional one, yeah okay.

"How exactly was I unprofessional?" Farren asked slowly.

"You let your personal feelings get in the way of what we were trying to accomplish," Evan stated. "You tried to undermine my authority in front of the band as well as my guest."

His guest? I guess he's talking about Botox Barbie groupie extraordinaire... He is out of his damn mind.

Before Farren could respond, Evan continued, "I talked to Mark already about disciplinary action, but he suggested a conversation about your behavior." He rolled his eyes dramatically.

Farren wouldn't cuss his ass out. She wouldn't fly off the handle like she suspected he wanted her to do with this asinine conversation. She would stay calm and think rationally.

I will stay calm; I will stay calm... Farren mentally repeated.

"I disagree with your view of the situation. I'm glad you brought this to my attention. I see now that I will need to take the necessary steps with Human Resources."

Farren wasn't bluffing. Her camera was already set-up and rolling and caught Evan's little power display on video. He was the unprofessional one, and she had proof.

"Now wait just a minute. There's no need to go to HR about this." Evan's eyes held a look of panic.

Farren knew then that *he* was the one bluffing.

"I think there is a very big need to go to HR. As a matter of fact, I'm feeling uncomfortable with this conversation, and I think I need to go. I'm sure we can meet at another time with a third party to discuss this."

Farren sashayed from the office with her packed bag. *If he thought he was going to bully me, he doesn't know who he's fuckin' with.*

———

Farren met Benny in the lobby. She was still staying with Eden and Camedon, and he stayed in the security booth at the station while she worked. She wasn't sure who got him access to the security office, but she was thankful. Benny would sit in the security office while she worked, and then he would escort her to the car and drive her home. Ever since the close call with the murderer, she felt grateful for Benny.

Farren had been super jumpy since the night she saw the murderer who she called *the creeper*. They still didn't know who he was. It was like he was a ghost. However, she knew Jones was working hard to find the guy, so until they had an actual name, he was simply referred to as *the creeper*.

It had been a long day at the radio station, especially after her little run-in with Evan, and she was ready to get back to the penthouse and rest. However, she had a meeting with Detective Carson. She couldn't understand why they would wait so long to contact her again, but she made sure to protect herself and what she saw. The night after the murder, Jones had taken a recording of her detailed description of what happened. They made copies and sent one to Jones' lawyer friend, Tyshawn Washington, and the others were locked in two different locations. Ms. Washington was one of the leading defense attorneys in not only the state, but the nation.

Jones wanted the lawyer at the meeting with Farren and the detective, but Farren thought it was overkill and extremely unnecessary. She had already met with the detectives, during which Ms. Washington had accompanied her. Once they saw they couldn't bully her, the interview went smoothly, and she had even worked with a sketch artist.

After Farren pointed out that fact, Jones relented. However, if his lawyer wasn't going to be in attendance, he insisted that he was there for the interview, and Farren didn't argue. She felt comforted by the fact that she wouldn't have to go through this process alone.

"Hey FB, you doing okay back there?" Benny questioned glancing at her through the rearview mirror.

"I'm okay, B-nice. Just been a long couple of weeks." Farren managed a weak smile for her new friend.

They had become close over the past few weeks. They even managed to give each other nicknames just like Farren had predicted.

Benny was a few years older than Farren, and an implant from New York. When she asked him how he came to work for Jones and Camedon, he simply smirked and said if he told her, he would have to kill her. Farren laughed, but something in the depths of his brown eyes told her he was only partially joking.

"Alright kiddo, we're here. Call me if you need me any more tonight," Benny said with a bright smile on his smooth, mahogany face.

"Benny, you're like three years older than me. What's with the kiddo?" Farren questioned as her face broke into a bright smile.

"No disrespect, FB. You just remind me of my younger sister. Kiddo is just another nickname." Benny gave Farren a wink as she nodded. "Anyway, give me a call if you need me," Benny said again.

"That's okay, Benny. Jones is coming by, so I think I'll be good for the rest of the night."

"If you're with Sullivan, I doubt being good is on the list of things he has in store," Benny remarked with a devilish smile. Farren couldn't help the heat that rose up in her cheeks.

In the past few weeks, she and Jones had become extremely close, and although they shared a few stolen kisses, they hadn't done any of the wicked things Jones had a reputation for. Hell, she'd been secretly hoping he would suggest they go to Club Euphoria, but no such luck. Jones was keeping their budding relationship PG13, and it was killing her.

Farren waved at Benny as she made her way inside her temporary home. She smiled at the doorman and entered the elevator. Her thoughts were on Jones, but lately, that seemed to be a reoccurring theme. As the elevator doors smoothly opened, she stepped into the penthouse. For the first time in forever, it was actually quiet. Harper had disappeared to wherever he went when he left Dallas for weeks at a time, Eden was meeting her parents and sister for dinner, and Camedon was getting Club Euphoria ready for their annual masquerade event. Farren was certain that Jones should've been helping with the event, but for some reason, he insisted on being there with her.

She had to admit the attention Jones gave her was flattering, and the lustful looks he gave her was bound to melt her panties at some point, but for some reason, he was hesitating. She had come to terms with the unbridled attraction she had for him, and with a little help from her friends, she accepted the fact that she wanted to see where things could go between them.

Farren plopped down on her bed to relax before the detective came, and she began to reminisce.

"Farren, girl if you want that foine ass Jones, I suggest you get on that before somebody else scoops that tall drink of deliciousness up." Farren couldn't say she was shocked at Elyse's words, but the fact that she said them out loud surprised the hell out of her.

"If I don't, are you going to scoop him up? Cause it sounds like you're a little more than interested," Farren questioned with a smirk.

"Yeah right!" Eden cackled pointing at her twin. "Like she would ever look at anyone besides Harper. Please."

"Shut up Eden. Nobody asked you." Elyse crossed her arms over her chest with a huff like a petulant child. "You ain't lookin' at nobody but Cam."

"Damn right." Eden responded with a wide smile.

Farren, Eden, and the twin's cousin, Maleeka laughed loudly at Elyse's pouting.

"It's obvious you want him, Farren. So what's the problem? I know you're not still stuck on that 'I can't date outside my race' bullshit." Elyse questioned.

"There's nothing wrong with preferring to date and marry a black man, Elyse." Maleeka chastised her cousin.

"I didn't say there was anything wrong with black men. Hell, I love me a fine piece of chocolate just like the next sista, but there's nothing wrong with a little vanilla either. If Farren wants Jones, then she should give him a chance. Color be damned!"

"Who said anything about me wanting Jones?" Farren asked with mock outrage.

All three ladies laughed in Farren's face. "Bihha, please. It is so obvious you want that man; I'm surprised he hadn't already seduced you into his dungeon." Elyse laughed.

Farren's body heated at the thought. She wondered if Jones actually had a dungeon and if he would spank her, oh the freaky things she could do in a sex dungeon.

"You are so nasty." Eden laughed, and Farren knew her naughty thoughts were written all over her face.

"So? You nasty too, heffa." Farren responded laughing. Eden had told her all about her raunchy episodes at Club Euphoria. Farren felt kind of guilty that she hadn't told her bestie about her special night at the club herself.

"Whateva, heffa," Eden laughed back. "But really Farren, Jones is a terrific guy. You shouldn't let his race deter you from giving him a chance."

Farren sighed. "This could all be a moot point anyway. He seems to be hesitating for some reason. The only thing he has done is kissed me until my panties were moist, and then he leaves me high and wet."

The girls chuckled.

"I know Jones is known for being... well, Jones. But it's different with you, Farren. He knows you. Maybe you need to tell him or better yet show him how interested you are in him." Eden said with a thoughtful expression.

And with that bit of advice, Farren decided that the next time they were alone, she would indeed show Jones just how interested she was.

––––––––

MURDERER

The buffoons at the Dallas Metro PD were going to cause him to kill somebody else. His pale blue eyes narrowed at the man sitting in front of him. He was an officer, a decorated one, and as dirty as they came. And he was going to do what needed to be done to get the Ryan case closed... asap.

"Detective, why haven't you closed in on the killer of Mr. Ryan?" His pale blue eyes became slits that relayed his disgust.

"Sir, Mr. Ryan had a lot of enemies. We don't have evidence connecting anyone to the murder," the detective said solemnly.

"This case needs to be closed... yesterday. The high profile is causing havoc in this great city. You need to find a suspect, and I don't care where you have to dig him up from. Understood?"

"Understood, sir. We will have a suspect by the end of the day."

"Good, good. Now make sure you have witness, and make that shit sticks. I don't have time for this bullshit right now."

Chapter Eleven

JONES

Jones finally felt like himself again. In fact, he was better than ever. The guilt that he had been feeling over Camedon's blackmail was no longer a nagging cloud hanging over his head. He was laughing more, and even though he had the daunting task of finding a murderer, Jones was happier than he'd been in a long time.

He owed all his renewed sense of self to one person: Farren. They had been hanging out and getting to know one another, and the more he was around her, the more joyous and relaxed he became. However, spending so much time with her he became more and more possessive.

How could he not feel like she was his? The mere thought of anyone else having her attention the way he did made his blood pressure rise.

Her happy-go-lucky attitude and sunny disposition sucked him in like a moth to a flame. But it was that naughtiness that simmered just below the surface of Farren's honey brown eyes that ultimately drew Jones to her. The mischievous smile, the effortlessly seductive way she moved, the teasing way she bit her plump bottom lip after a sassy retort. The sway of her bountiful hips. She was both the joy while simultaneously being the torture in his life.

Jones had been trying something different with Farren. She wasn't just some chick that he wanted to have sex with. She was somebody that he wanted to get to know and have around. It was hell trying to keep his hands to himself with her giving him the "come and get it" looks. However, he knew she was worth the wait.

"Hey Savanah, I'm going to head out. Text or call if anything comes up," Jones said to his assistant on his way out of his office.

"Umm. Did you forget about your meeting?" Savanah nervously responded.

Shit, Jones thought. He actually did forget, but he wasn't going to leave Farren alone to be interviewed by some incompetent detective.

"Can you push the meeting back? Let the clients know that we will meet at Euphoria, and tell Monique to show them around." Jones knew that the guys at the Simon Group wanted to make an investment in their company, and he and Camedon had plans for Euphoria, so by meeting them at the club, he would be killing two birds with one stone.

"Yes, sir. I can do that," Savanah answered with a visible relief on her pretty face.

Jones nodded and left the office. He was dead set on getting to Camedon's apartment before the detective showed up.

Jones made it to Camedon's place in record time. He hated that Farren wouldn't agree to let his attorney friend be there when the police questioned her again. He didn't like the way the detective had questioned her the first time. He'd treated Farren like a suspect, and Jones didn't like that at all.

As Jones exited his vehicle and made his way to the private elevator, his focus was on one thing, getting to Farren.

The elevator dinged, breaking his concentration and signaling his arrival to the penthouse apartment. Jones cautiously made his way to the sitting area. When he didn't see anyone, he made his way to the guest room where Farren was staying.

"Farren? Are you here?" Jones called out, making his way down the winding hallway. Jones quickened his pace, but when he got outside of her door, he paused when he heard her moan. Now, under normal circumstances, the sounds coming from her room would turn him on, but at this particular moment, her moans were out of place.

Why would she be moaning? Is she having sex when she should be expecting the detective? Is the detective in there with her?

"Farren!" Jones' loud voice carried through the empty hall.

"Jones?" Farren's breathy reply from the other-side of the door made Jones suspicious.

He wasn't sure what was going on, but by the sound of her voice it sounded like she was in the throes of passion.

Did he really want to walk in on her if she was with someone? Could the rage he was felling be quelled? He loved to watch her, and he knew that from her display at Euphoria, but could he stand it if she was with someone else? Could he ever replace the image?

Jones shook the thoughts from his head and twisted the doorknob. If she was with someone else, he would deal with it...somehow.

When he barged into the room, Farren was pulling on a robe. Her face was flushed, and she was looking everywhere but him.

"Jones? What are you doing here?"

Jones looked around the room. Farren was the only one there. He scanned the space from left to right and top to bottom, his eyes shifting quickly to the bathroom door which stood open. There was nobody there.

"I came for the interview. That was today, right?" Jones questioned his brows furrowed. Maybe he got the days mixed up somehow.

"Oh. Uh, it was cancelled. The detective called to reschedule. I texted you." Farren looked down sheepishly, her face becoming more flushed. "I, uh..."

Jones' face split into a devious grin. He knew what she was up to in her room before he got there. He only wished he would've just come in without calling her name first. Jones knew it probably made him a pervert, but he would give anything to see Farren caressing herself to completion like she did before.

"I'm sorry. Was I interrupting something?" Jones injected as much innocence as he could muster into his question.

"No. Um. I was... uh... about to hop in the shower." Farren stammered, still not making eye contact.

Jones smiled. He wasn't sure why Farren was acting so embarrassed when he knew for a fact that she was an exhibitionist. Maybe it was because Farren thought her exhibitionism was a secret.

Jones decided to have mercy on her and change the subject before she blushed so hard that her body went up in actual flames.

"So since the detective isn't here, why don't I take you out for a bite to eat?"

Farren let out a deep, audible breath, and Jones knew from the sound that she was relieved that he didn't question her any further.

"Yeah, that sounds great. Just let me take that shower and we can go." Farren's round shaped face held a relieved smile, but her skin still held red undertones from her earlier embarrassment.

"Alright. I'll just wait in the living room. Unless you need help... or you want me to watch?" Jones smiled boldly at Farren as the look of disbelief crossed her face. He wanted to see if she would question his word choice. Jones wanted to find out if she would be bold enough to ask him what he meant.

"Watch?" Farren's face held no confusion even though she questioned his meaning. Her eyes told on her; they flickered with lust and desire. "No, I don't need you to watch," she finally answered as she sashayed into the bathroom. Before she reached the inside, she shot a seductive look over her shoulder and said, "At least not yet." The smile she graced him with before she shut the bathroom door was devilish in all the right ways.

———

Twenty minutes later, Farren emerged from her room smelling good and looking delicious. Her body was wrapped in a black silky jumpsuit, and it complemented her skin making the cinnamon undertones stand out. Her hair was pulled back, making her neck look long and delicate. She was absolutely stunning.

"You look beautiful, Farren." Jones smiled as he stood and kissed her on the side of her mouth. He couldn't resist the temptation her cherry colored lips were presenting.

Her face broke into a slow, provocative grin. "Thank you, Jones."

"Shall we go?" Jones gave her a slow, lascivious smile with a tilt of his head toward the door.

Farren nodded, and he placed his hand on the small of her back as he guided her to the elevator. With the outfit that she had chosen, and the sounds coming from her room earlier, Jones knew that tonight, he wouldn't be able to resist Farren. He would give in to his cardinal desires, and he had to be honest with himself... he couldn't wait.

The night had flown by, and before Jones' knew it, it was time for his meeting. He didn't want the night with Farren to end, so he decided he would press his luck.

"I need to go to Euphoria for a meeting..." Jones started looking deep into Farren's beautiful bright eyes.

"Oh. Okay, well thanks for dinner. I had a good time. Did you need me to call Benny for a ride?" Farren questioned with what sounded like disappointment.

"No. I want you to come with me to Euphoria." Jones wasn't giving her an option. There was no more cat and mouse. It was time to take off the kid gloves and show Farren who he really was. It wasn't like she didn't know already. He might as well give her a first-hand view.

A slow sensual smile broke out on Farren's face. "Well, it's about damn time," she said with a sassy wink.

Jones couldn't help the salacious smile that lit up his face even if he wanted to, and he damn sure didn't want to.

"I was wondering when I would meet *The* Jones Sullivan everyone has been warning me about. So you ready to go?" she questioned with a saucy smile.

"I knew the naughty vixen I watched at Euphoria was in there somewhere. I've been waiting too." Jones winked, and his smile grew at the wide-eyed stare Farren was throwing his way.

"What do you mean... the vixen *you watched?*" Farren questioned, her eyes narrowing slightly.

"You know *exactly* what I mean." Jones' voice was low and husky, revealing his dark lust.

There's no hiding now... the gloves are off.

Chapter Twelve

FARREN

"You know *exactly* what I mean."

I know damn well Jones hasn't seen me in any type of sexual capacity. Well, except for earlier when he almost caught me masturbating, but that doesn't count. Shit! He must've seen me at Euphoria. Farren's thoughts were racing as she tried to figure out Jones' not so subtle remarks.

The nervousness that was bubbling up in Farren tried its hardest to come out, but she held it at bay as she tried her best to make her voice stern and steady. "No, really Jones... what are you talking about, and don't play with me."

"Listen Farren, we've known each other for quite some time now." Jones paused as if he was trying to choose his words carefully. "Well, we've at least been around each other, even if you don't know me very well. But I promise you, I would never bring up what was done in the privacy of Euphoria in passing conversation. I'm not that type of man. Besides, that's not how we run our club."

Farren was taken aback by his words. Jones never mentioned that he saw her at Euphoria. After the first couple of times she met him and Camedon, and neither of them said anything about her being at the club, she assumed they never saw her, or at the very least they didn't recognize her without a mask.

"Well, I guess I can trust you with my secrets." Farren smirked, trying to cover her feelings of uneasiness.

"Indeed, you definitely can." Jones affectionately smiled at her.

"I've only been there a couple of times, with an ex of mine. Eden has no idea..."

Before Farren could finish her rambling explanation, Jones held his hand up to stop her verbal diarrhea. "There's no need to explain. Like I said, I would never divulge your private business to anyone. That includes your *best friend*." Jones' raised eyebrow told Farren that he was curious as to why Eden didn't know about her extracurricular activities, but she wasn't about to spill that tea.

"Thanks. I guess we should get going to the club then?" she questioned, changing the subject.

"Yes, ma'am we should." Jones nodded as he stood to help her from her seat.

Farren couldn't help the hitch in her breathing when Jones helped her from her chair, and placed his large warm hand to the small of her back. His touch always did something to her. Farren couldn't figure out if it was the fact that she knew Jones' reputation for not giving a damn, doing exactly what he wanted, or the fact that he was so damn sexy that he could charm anyone to do just about anything.

He escorted her to the waiting car, and she could feel the envious stares of women in the restaurant. Hell, she would be jealous too if she wasn't on the receiving end of his affection. Jones was the epitome of sexy with his dark gray suit, and the casual way he wore his fitted white dress shirt with the top buttons undone. His auburn hair was parted on the side with the longer top swept back away from his striking hazel eyes. His strong jaw was covered in a dusting of dark red hair that made his full pink lips stand out.

I am indeed a lucky woman! Farren thought as she put a little more sway to her full hips.

Once she was in the car, Farren couldn't help the nervous excitement that was radiating off of her. She hadn't been to Euphoria in several months, and now to be going with Jones Sullivan of all people, she had no idea what to expect.

It seemed like it took hours to get to Euphoria, when in actuality it probably only took twenty minutes at the most. Farren's heart was pounding loudly in her ears. The anticipation of being in such an erotic place made excitement flow through her veins.

The last time Farren ventured into Euphoria with her ex-boyfriend, Erick, he convinced her to let loose and try something outside of her comfort zone. Being at the club itself was something that Farren was very comfortable with. The anonymity of the mask she was wearing and the fact that everyone in the exclusive club shared the same secret desires and fantasies made her feel relaxed. However, Erick had wanted her to explore more of herself, so he showed her a room where she was surrounded by mirrors. He told her that in this room, she could lose her inhibitions, explore and touch her body while she watched her reflection. He wanted *her* to see how sexy she was.

Erick explained that the mirrors were two-way and he would be on the other side watching her. Farren knew subconsciously that Erick wouldn't be the only person that could see her, and that made the act that much more exciting. She took off her mask, stripped seductively, and pleasured herself like never before all the while looking at one mirror in particular. Farren had felt like someone was watching her intently from the other side, and she had felt it in her bones that this sexy show was not just for her. However, she had no idea that the person watching was Jones of all people.

"Would you like a mask?" Jones asked, breaking into Farren's thoughts.

"Are you wearing one?" She was curious of what the night entailed and if wearing a mask would be beneficial.

"Not tonight," Jones replied with a blank expression.

"Oh," was all Farren could say, the disappointment evident in her voice. Did that mean he wasn't going to have a little fun with her after all?

"This evening I'm here for a meeting, and although it's about business tonight, the next time I bring you here, it won't be." Jones' eyes held hers with a feverish desire that couldn't be denied.

Farren swallowed an audible gulp. She was so turned on by the passionate look that she almost lost her train of thought. "Uh... if you're here for a meeting, why did you bring me?"

"Because I wasn't ready for our night to end," he answered simply.

Farren nodded, but she still wasn't quite sure what she was supposed to do while he had this mysterious meeting.

"So while you're in your meeting, what am I supposed to be doing?" Farren asked with an arched brow.

"You're going to be by my side watching the entertainment." The smile he gave her was downright criminal.

———

Being whisked into the club through a private entrance by huge body-guards surrounding them, Farren felt like she was in a James Bond movie. She had only been to Euphoria a couple of times before, but she had no idea the back entrance even existed.

I guess if you're hanging with the boss, you're even more exclusive in the most exclusive club in town, Farren thought as she took in all the security they passed going into the club. It seemed after the break-in, and the recent trouble Euphoria had, they beefed up the security measures even more than before.

The bodyguards who seemingly came out of nowhere led them through a long narrow hallway and up a flight of stairs. When they reached yet another entrance, a keycard was used to open the large door. Once they were inside, they were lead to a sizeable private room where four gentlemen and three ladies were waiting.

The men were all dressed in suits, and like Jones, they weren't wearing ties. The ladies that accompanied them were all dressed in slinky club attire. The men all got up out of their seats when they entered the room, and the gesture made Farren smile.

Farren once again scanned her surroundings, taking in the sumptu-ousness of the room. The dark walls and flooring that were accented with whiskey colored furniture made Farren feel like she was inside of an old mansion's study. The dim lighting of the chandelier, as well as several lamps and floor lights, created a warm glow throughout the space. All that was needed was a cigarette girl, and Farren would've felt like she entered a 1920's cigar club.

"Hello, Sullivan." A tall, handsome man with dark eyes stepped forward to greet Jones. His mysterious eyes strayed toward Farren, and she couldn't read the emotion that was held in them.

"Parsons. Nice of you to meet me here. Sorry for the inconvenience." Farren noticed that Jones' voice was flat, and his face was blank when he responded.

"I'm Alexander Parsons, and who might you be?" The man stepped in Farren's direction looking at her intently.

Farren gave a courteous smile, but Alexander gave her the creeps. As she got a better look, his dark eyes didn't hold a bit of anything in their depths, and she sure didn't want to find out just why that was.

"This is my girlfriend... baby, why don't you go with Monique and get us some drinks? She'll show you around, and when you get back, I'll make this inconvenience up to you," Jones stated as he put himself in between Alexander and her. Farren wasn't sure why Jones didn't want her to be introduced to the man, but she definitely wasn't upset about it.

"Sure, *babe*. Can I get you your usual?" Farren asked pleasantly, but she knew that Jones wasn't fooled. He had some explaining to do.

"Yes." Then he pulled Farren into his body and laid a kiss on her so passionate that she was sure if she were wearing panties, they would've melted right off her body. Although they had kissed several times before, she wasn't sure why he decided to kiss her so daringly in front of his business associates.

Yeah! He definitely has some explaining to do, she thought as he released her from his kiss. Farren stumbled slightly before righting herself with a blush. Jones simply gave her his charming smile and pecked her gently on the lips before sending her on her way.

Farren mindlessly followed Monique to get drinks. She had no idea what to expect, but this night seemed to get more and more interesting as it went on. When she looked over her shoulder, she caught a glimpse of Jones watching her walk away with a lustful look on his face. Farren knew exactly how she wanted this night to end.

It looks like Jones is going to be my trip into swirl nation after all.

Chapter Thirteen

JONES

Jones watched Farren sashay away, and when she looked back over her shoulder, he smiled wickedly. If she thought he was going to look away, she was crazy. There was no way in hell he was going to pretend not to see that glorious view. No. Way. In. Hell!

"It's unlike you, Sullivan, to bring a woman around. Who is she really?" Alexander questioned, his gaze staring after Farren as well.

Jones didn't dislike Alexander Parsons. He just knew what type of man he was. Parsons was a ruthless cutthroat business man who went after what he wanted. He was unpredictable and rude which was the reason he intervened when he saw the interest in Farren light up in the man's eyes.

"We're here for business, so let's get down to what we came here for," Jones stated dismissively, walking toward the other men in the group.

The meeting was informal because of the location, but the topic of conversation was still a serious one. The Simon Group was a private entity that invested in properties throughout the country. Like Jones and Camedon, they kept their holdings exclusive. The group was looking to make an investment that would expand Euphoria to different cities throughout the nation, and then globally if everything went according to plan.

"So you gentlemen have seen Euphoria. What do you think?" Jones asked the men after they settled into their comfortable leather chairs.

"The venue is more than I expected. I like that the building is inconspicuous," one man commented.

All the men nodded in agreement with their colleague. Jones knew that they were trying to keep their excitement to a minimum, but he could read the enthusiasm in their eyes.

"Yes, we want to keep our business exclusive. We don't want or need a neon sign flashing what we have going on here."

The men all nodded and chuckled their agreement.

"Based on what Monique was kind enough to show us, your clientele seems very relaxed and willing to spend their money."

"Yes, we make sure that our members feel free to be themselves. The more comfortable they are, the more they're willing to spend to be here." Jones didn't really have to convince the men that what he and Camedon had going was a success. The business really sold itself.

"Makes sense," Parsons added.

"This is definitely a venture we want to look more into," a man by the name of Jonathan Wright, who in Jones' opinion was the person who made all the decisions, said. Even though Parsons did most of the talking.

After another twenty minutes of discussion, Monique and Farren returned with drinks in hand. Farren gave Jones a shy smile as their gazes locked.

"Well gentlemen, Monique will give you a tour of the rest of the facility." Jones rose from his seat and extended his hand to Jonathan. They shook, and the men began to follow Monique out of the room.

"I'll have my assistant, Marsha, call Savanah and set-up a meeting for later this week," Jonathan remarked on his way out the door.

Jones nodded. He was excited that the group wanted to invest. Jones and Camedon could make an exorbitant amount of money on the deal, and when Jonathan set-up an additional meeting that meant they were ready to make an offer.

Alexander lingered in the room after the other men had vacated.

Jones didn't want a confrontation with the man, especially if they were going into business, but the man was uncouth, so there was no telling what was going to come out of his mouth.

"Sullivan, this is a real classy establishment you all have here. I was wondering about the personal benefits of this investment. As an elite member of the investment team, does that come with an exclusive membership?"

Jones didn't have any intention of having this conversation with Parsons. Membership was exclusive, but with an investment the Simon Group would potentially make, of course the membership would be offered.

However, there wouldn't be any offer until the ink was dry, and the money was in the bank.

"That will all be discussed during contract negotiations with my partner. Now if you don't mind, I have a lovely lady that needs my attention." Jones watched Parsons give a tight nod but hesitated as if he was going to say something else. Before Parsons could speak, Jones turned away, effectively dismissing the other man.

Now that the business portion of his night was over, he could spend the rest of his time seducing Farren. He could sense that she was excited about coming to Euphoria, but Jones could also tell she was disappointed they wouldn't be engaging in any of the *activities* that the club had to offer.

———

"So Ms. Bell, what would you like to see first?" Jones questioned in a low seductive voice in Farren's ear.

He was close enough to see the goosebumps appear on her smooth skin. Jones loved the feel of her skin, and the soft smell of her perfume. He could simply caress and kiss her all over her body from head to toe and be a satisfied man.

"Well, you brought me here for a little naughtiness, so let's see what we can get into." The smile that Farren gave him was one of the sexiest smiles he had ever seen.

Jones took her by the hand and led her down a short hallway to an elevator. He pushed the down button as they boarded and the sexual tension that surrounded the small space was electrifying. Jones stepped off the elevator with Farren in tow and led her to a room that she wouldn't recognize, but one that he would never forget. It was where he'd first laid eyes on her.

The room was occupied with several couples in various stages of undress, and the *show* was already in full swing. Instead of a solo act like when Farren was in the room, there were two couples.

Jones led Farren to a secluded section in the front of the room that was reserved specifically for him. Although the lighting in the circular shaped room was dim, he could see the fire in Farren's eyes. He watched her closely as she sunk slowly into her seat, her eyes never leaving the two couples in front of them.

A blonde woman was straddling the face of her partner, rotating her hips over his mouth and tongue in a slow sensual motion while she kissed the other woman passionately. The brunette woman kissed and nibbled at the blonde woman's mouth as her partner took her from behind. His strokes were long and slow matching the rhythm of the blonde woman's rotating hips. It was like a perfectly choreographed dance between the four of them that began to get more and more zealous as time wore on.

Farren and Jones were sitting so close that their thighs were brushing. Farren seemed mesmerized by the raw and dirty sounds that were drowning out any music that was playing. Jones watched as she slowly licked her lips, the motion leaving a moist trail on her now glistening mouth.

Jones loved a good show as much as the next man, but the people engaged in some of the nastiest acts he'd ever seen couldn't hold his attention. His gaze never strayed from the beauty sitting next to him. Her breathing picked up and her breasts moved up and down at a rapid pace. Her nipples pebbled under the curve hugging fabric, and he couldn't help the pool of moisture that settled in his mouth at the sight. Jones watched as Farren squeezed her luscious thighs together, and all he wanted to do was pry them apart and dive into the heaven he knew awaited him there.

Jones slid his hand up her juicy thigh, and without turning away, she parted the gates to heaven. He slowly and methodically rubbed his large slightly calloused hand from her knee toward his prize. He squeezed her inner thigh as he worked his way upwards. The silky fabric of the jumpsuit helped glide his hand smoothly.

Jones only wished he could feel her skin; he knew that it would be covered in goosebumps. The closer he got to her center, the hotter she felt. He could practically feel the heat radiating off her body. He inched his way closer and as soon as he was about to have some fun, Farren clamped her strong thighs on his hand in a vise.

She slowly turned her head to face him. "Did you think it was going to be that easy, Mr. Sullivan?"

He smirked. "Nothing is ever easy with you, Ms. Bell."

Jones leaned over and took her mouth in a slow kiss. His tongue probed her warm, slick mouth. He could taste the cranberry from the drink she had earlier. She moaned into his mouth and scooted closer, pressing her body against his. Jones wrapped his strong arms around her and grabbed the back of her neck with his hand. He devoured her lips, sucking and biting on her full bottom lip wanting, needing more of her.

Farren whimpered as she broke the kiss. She took a deep breath, sat back, and crossed one long leg over the other with a smile spread across her beautiful face.

"We're just getting to the climax of the show. You don't want to miss the best part, do you?" Farren questioned huskily.

Jones took a deep breath trying to get himself under control. He wasn't normally a man to play cat and mouse games, but with Farren, he would play any type of game she wanted. He sat back and crossed his ankle over his knee. He wouldn't let her see him sweat.

"Anything you want, Sugar." He smiled charmingly.

Chapter Fourteen

FARREN

Farren sat with her legs tightly crossed. She closed her eyes an inhaled. She had to get herself together. If Jones didn't stop caressing and kissing her, she definitely was going to show him a real good time. In fact, she was going to show him a whole other world if he kept up his seduction. She wasn't too dense to see that he was seducing the hell out of her.

She had been moist since he kissed her the first time. Now, she was scared to move because she just knew her silky jumpsuit would tell all of her womanly secrets. Farren tried to focus on something other than the gorgeous man beside her, but they were in a sex club for goodness sakes. Everywhere she looked, she saw something that turned her on.

There wasn't any point in her trying to fight her desires any longer. Farren was a strong, bold, and independent woman. She was single and unattached, and at this moment, there wasn't a single reason that she could think to keep her from devouring Mr. Jones Sullivan.

Farren inhaled deeply once more to gather her courage. She turned her head and her honey brown eyes connected to his golden hazel ones. His eyes were blazing with the passion she was feeling inside of her. Farren leaned forward and slowly licked his plush bottom lip. He tasted like whiskey and masculinity. His taste intoxicated her. She teasingly bit his lip and the growl that erupted from his chest made her simultaneously quiver and moisten.

"The kid gloves are off, Ms. Bell. You sure you want to release this beast?" Jones' voice was deeper than Farren had ever heard it before. It was rich and dark like melted chocolate.

"Nobody asked you to use them in the first place, Mr. Sullivan."

Before Farren realized what happened, she was straddling Jones' lap. His hands had traveled down her back and before she knew it, he had her voluptuous ass in a death grip. It shouldn't have shocked her that he snatched her from her chair so fast her head was spinning. Hell, she didn't have time to process that she even moved.

"Shit, Farren! This ass..." Jones' voice was a low rumble.

Farren lost all control. Her heartrate sky rocketed, the moisture that surrounded her core was now a pool of desire as her body heated from the inside out.

"I really liked this outfit, but I swear to God I am about to tear you out of this shit." Jones reached for the back of her jumpsuit to do just that, but when his words registered in her sluggish lust filled brain, she reluctantly stopped him.

"Whoa there, cowboy, it might be cool for me to prance my naked ass around this club, but I don't think the people outside of here will appreciate me in all my glory." Farren was able to reply with her usual sass, but her heart was beating in her ears so loud she could barely hear her own voice.

When Jones abruptly stood, all she could do was wrap her long legs around his waist. *Damn, he's strong! Fuck, that's sexy!* Farren couldn't form another coherent thought as Jones kissed her senseless.

"Let's get out of here then. Because I'm ripping this shit off you tonight."

"You know you could just take it off me," Farren stated, still breathless.

"What's the fun in that?" Jones questioned as he gently set Farren on her feet, and led her out of the club.

———

Inside of the chauffeured driven vehicle, Farren couldn't keep her hands off of Jones. Apparently, the feeling was mutual because somehow, she had ended up in his lap once again. But she couldn't bring herself to care; his body felt so good against hers. Everywhere she was soft, he was all man. The hard, muscled planes of his chest pressed against her soft breasts felt like heaven.

Farren was in mid-grind when she heard the tell-tale sound of soft fabric ripping. She abruptly stopped her movements.

"What the hell?!" she yelled out in protest.

Jones just continued to kiss her neck, ravishing her with frantic kisses. His hands found their way into the back of her now ripped jumpsuit to grab a hold of her ass.

"No panties. That's the type of shit I like!" Farren could feel the smirk of his glorious mouth against her neck.

"How am I going to get out of the car like..." Jones slipped his fingers into her dripping core from behind, and the questioned died a quiet death on her lips as a moan took over.

His fingers were pumping in and out at a steady leisurely pace. Farren squirmed and moaned as her breathing became shallower by the second.

Jones licked and sucked her neck, and then he moved fluidly to her mouth without breaking contact from her skin. His skilled fingers touched her with a gloriousness that she had never felt.

Farren could feel her climax building to the point of no return. Just a little more and she would fall over the cliff into blissful pleasure. She rotated her hips faster, but then the pressure of Jones' prodding masterful fingers began to lessen. And then without warning, he removed his touch from her all together, depriving her of the climax she so desperately needed.

What the hell?!

Farren drew back to look into his face to see why in the ever-loving hell he had stopped. But she was blinded by the sight of Jones' slipping his drenched fingers into his mouth. He seemed to relish her flavor, moaning his pleasure before he slowly opened his smoldering hazel eyes.

"Best fuckin' thing I've ever tasted." His voice was now gravelly, and lust filled.

Damn that was sexy as hell! What am I supposed to say to that?

Jones leaned up and kissed her lips quickly before taking off his jacket. He maneuvered it off smoothly even with her still draped over his lap.

"Put this on, baby. We're here."

Farren looked around, and quickly realized that they were at Jones' place. She had been so wanton that she didn't even realize the car had stopped moving. If she had any shame left, she would feel embarrassed. But she didn't. Farren was about to have some of the best sex of her life. And she was positive it was going to be good because the way Jones kissed was a magic she'd never experienced before.

Chapter Fifteen

JONES

Damn, this woman was going to be the death of him. He wanted to keep his fingers in his mouth until he could no longer taste her. Farren's sweet and tangy flavor on his lips had him wanting to tear the rest of her outfit to shreds, and pound into her heat like a savage in the back of the car.

He couldn't help himself once he got a hold of her luscious ass, and before he knew what was happening, his control had slipped, and he was getting to her pussy by any means necessary. Hearing the rip of the barrier of fabric that was in his way was music to his ears. He was so lost in touching her smooth skin that he almost told the driver to keep driving, but he didn't want to roll down the partition and break the connection from Farren. Jones would just have to keep the rest of his sanity, and wait to devour her when he got her home.

Jones moved with an unhurried stride through his building's lobby. Like the very first time he brought Farren here, he held her hand in reassurance. He knew this was a big step for them and everything would be different after tonight. However, there was no turning back. He wanted her more than he had ever wanted a woman before.

As they stepped onto the elevator, he breathed a sigh of relief. It would only be a few more minutes, and they would be in his apartment. He was so close to throwing her over his shoulder and running through the lobby like a ragging lunatic, but he kept it together long enough to make it to his place.

They entered his home and as the door shut behind them, Jones' control snapped. He tore his jacket from around her shoulders, and slung it to the floor. Farren hastily undid the halter top of her jumpsuit, and revealed her golden-brown breasts to him.

Jones stalked forward until her back was up against the wall. He grabbed her wrists in his hand and held them above her head. She arched her beautiful breasts out, and he wanted to consume all of her. Farren's gorgeous cinnamon skin was heated, her lids were heavy with desire, and her plump lips were swollen from his kisses. She looked absolutely stunning.

Jones attacked the protruding buds of her heavy globes that pebbled just for him. He lavished her breasts with licks and sucks making her beg him for more. There was so much he wanted to do to her, but the time for play would come later. If he didn't get into her wet core now, he was certain death awaited him.

Jones stripped off the rest of her ragged jumpsuit. *I'm going to have to replace that. It was a sexy outfit on her*, he thought as he watched the fabric fall softly from her body.

Damn, she looks breathtaking. He shook his head in disbelief. He finally had Farren where he wanted her.

Jones stepped back and dropped his hands. "Don't move. Keep your hands above your head."

Farren frowned slightly, but she stayed against the wall with her hands above her head, her tattered jumpsuit gathered around her ankles, her high heels still on her feet.

Jones bent down and removed her shoes and the jumpsuit. He threw them to the side as he stood up. He took a moment to take in her deliciously naked form. He ran his finger down the valley of her breasts. "Damn... you look so fucking good."

Jones lowered himself down on his knees, his face right in front of the golden heaven of Farren's heated core. He leaned forward and inhaled deeply. Her scent was intoxicating. He took a long deep lick, once again relishing her taste on his tongue. He licked and sucked at her lower lips as he circled his tongue, putting pressure on her clit.

Farren gave a throaty moan, and that was all he could take of the foreplay.

"I'm going to need you to hold on tight."

That was all the warning Jones gave her. He unzipped his pants and pulled out his hard as steel pipe in one swift motion. He thrust into her deeply and without mercy.

Jones wanted to play it cool, he wanted to be gentle, he wanted to take his time. But once he felt the smoothness of her silky dripping wet walls grip his dick, it was over.

The blissful sounds that was coming from this vixen wrapped around him was driving him to the brink of his sanity. The walls of her channel tightened and tugged at his rod, pulsating gloriously with each pound of his hips.

"Shit, Farren! This pussy...uh... so good." Jones couldn't control the hoarseness of his voice. He was hanging on by a thread, but he would give her the pleasure she needed before he came. He slowed down his movements, but it wasn't long before his pace kicked up and he was back to pounding into her.

"I need you to come, baby. Let go for me." Jones ground his pelvis into hers on a mission.

Farren thrashed and moaned as she moved with him. She equaled his every stroke, and it confirmed what he suspected; she was his match.

Jones continued to thrust into her. He was lost in the feel of her soft, glorious body. He knew right then if Farren ever tried to take away her sweetness, he would stalk her ass.

His thrusts were precise; he gave her what she wanted, and exactly what he needed. Jones found the bundle of nerves that made her quake, and he hit it over and over again. The feel of her pussy fluttering around his shaft was driving him crazy. He pressed her harder against the wall, pistoning his hips with abandonment until he felt a gush of wetness from her core.

"Ummm... Jones, I'm coming, don't stop!" Farren loudly cried out, her thighs tightening their hold on him.

Jones didn't answer. In fact, he couldn't. All he could manage was a grunt as he chased his own orgasm.

When Farren screamed out her release, Jones let go immediately after, moaning as his orgasm took over his body, filling her core with his essence. He held her against the wall as her body continued to shake. They were both breathing as if they'd run a marathon, both their chests were heaving, and sweat dripped from their sated bodies.

They stood locked in an embrace, staring at each other for what seemed like hours. Jones could've stood there all night looking into those beautiful soulful eyes. They were soft and held a look of utter satisfaction, and he couldn't bring himself to look away.

"We didn't use protection." Farren's soft spoken words broke the silence.

"I know." Jones lived a certain lifestyle, and he was always safe. He got tested regularly and always used protection. But he had to admit with Farren, he just didn't want to.

"I'm sorry that I didn't use protection with you, Farren. I sincerely apologize if I upset you... I'm clean, I have the papers if you want to see them."

Farren sighed but she didn't take her attention away from him, and for that Jones was grateful.

"Okay, but we need to talk about it... later though," Farren finally responded.

Jones kissed her swollen lips, "anything you want."

"Are you getting tired of holding me yet?" Farren graced him with a small smile breaking the slight awkwardness.

"Never." Jones gave her another quick kiss before he walked them from the living room to his bedroom. Farren was still in his arms with her legs wrapped around his waist, and him still buried deep inside of her.

Her boobs jiggled as he walked, and her nipples began to pebble, and that's all it took for his manhood to come back alive.

Farren's eyebrows rose high on her forehead. "Again?"

"Oh, come on now baby girl, you didn't think that was it did you?" Jones chuckled. "That was just a warm-up. I hope you don't have plans for tomorrow."

"Tomorrow?" Farren questioned with wide-eyes.

"Did you actually think once you gave me this pussy, I was going to be finished in one night?" Jones looked at her with a stern face as he shook his head.

What the hell is she thinking? I'm not letting her out of my bed for at least twenty-four hours.

————

Ringing... what the hell is that ringing? Jones groggily wiped his eyes. He was having the best sleep of his life, and he couldn't for the life of him figure out why his cell wouldn't stop ringing.

He grabbed the device to shut it off, when he noticed it wasn't his phone at all. It was Farren's.

They had made love for hours once they made it to his bedroom. After the third or fourth round, he was merciful enough to give her a break, not that he wanted to, but he knew that she had to be sore from all of their rigorous activity.

Jones had made them something to eat, and gathered all their discarded belongings and headed back to the bedroom. They ate and chatted well into the early morning hours before making love again before falling into a peaceful sleep.

Now the shrill ringing was messing up his good sleep.

"Babe, the phone." Jones groaned as he reached for her.

"Ugggg." He heard Farren moan as she kicked her legs like a toddler.

Finally, the ringing stopped only to start back up again. He felt Farren move and her hoarse voice whisper. "Hello?"

Jones could only hear one side of the conversation, but the way Farren started frantically moving around his room had him waking up instantly.

Once she disconnected the call, she plopped down on the bed with her head in her hands.

"What's going on?" Jones questioned as he pulled a shaking Farren into his massive arms.

"That was my apartment manager. Somebody broke into my house. My place is trashed."

"What?! Who in the hell would break into your house?"

"I don't know, but the police are there, and I need to go."

"Of course, baby, let me get dressed. I'll take care of this. You don't need to worry about anything. Okay?" Jones lifted her chin and kissed her lips softly.

"Uh... I would love to get dressed too... but you know, you kinda ripped my outfit like a caveman last night so." Farren looked at him with an arched brow.

"Shit! I totally forgot about that." Jones tried his best to look ashamed but failed miserably. The way he wanted to ravage her, that poor jumpsuit was just a casualty. In fact, he was proud that some of the outfit was still intact. It could've been much worse.

"You jump in the shower, and I'll have something brought up from the boutique downstairs."

"Well, that's mighty fancy of you." Farren gave him a smile, but he could tell that the break-in was getting to her.

"It will be okay, sweetheart. I promise." Jones gave Farren a tight hug and kissed her lips softly.

Farren sighed. "I know this has to do with the investigation. I just have this feeling."

Jones wanted to reassure her, but he knew that there was truth to what she said. Farren just had an interview with the detective on the murder investigation a few days prior, now all of a sudden there was a break-in at her house.

Jones wanted to believe this was some random crime, and for the sake of the detective working the case, it better be. Because if Farren's information got in the wrong hands, it was going to be hell to pay. But Jones knew it wasn't random, and he didn't believe in coincidences. He had a bad feeling that things just got real.

Chapter Sixteen

FARREN

After the glorious night she had, it was just her luck that someone would break into her house. She could barely bask in the afterglow of their magnificent sex before some bastard rained on her parade.

Fuck, I hate people sometimes! Farren sat sulking as she watched the scenery pass through the window. Benny was back on duty, and she felt comforted that she had both him and Jones by her side.

She couldn't help but think that Jones was right, and the Dallas Metro had a leak and the killer knew who she was. Was she in danger now? Was the man that murdered a guy in cold blood in her house? Was he looking for her?

All the questions plagued her mind and she couldn't keep her thoughts from going back to the interview she had a few days earlier with the two detectives Carson and Lawson.

"So Ms. Bell, are you positive it was a white man that you saw struggling with Peter Ryan that night in the alley?" Detective Carson questioned.

"Yes, I'm sure."

"And the man had," the detective paused while he searched his unorganized notes, *"pale blue eyes. And you're sure about that too?"* Carson questioned his expression said he didn't believe Farren, but she didn't care.

"I'm positive. I know what I saw. I know who I saw." Farren answered sharply.

"We just need to make sure, Ms. Bell. It's nothing personal. We just want to make sure we get the right guy who did this that's all." Detective Lawson interjected.

Farren felt as though Lawson was there to keep his partner in line. It was obvious that Carson didn't give a shit about her or the case.

"So you didn't recognize the perp or the victim at the time of the crime?" Detective Carson interrupted.

"No. I didn't know who the victim was until later. I've never seen the man who killed Mr. Ryan before." Farren answered honestly.

Lawson patted her hand in reassurance with a small smile, but Carson simply nodded his head. Farren could see that Carson was detached from the interview. It was like he was simply going through the motions and she had a feeling she was wasting her time.

"Did you get a hit on the drawing? I worked with your artist for hours, and it turned out really well. The man I saw had very distinctive eyes, somebody has had to see him before."

Carson gave a noncommittal shrug, and continued to scribble in his notepad. Farren was doing her best to stay calm, but his nonchalant attitude was pissing her off. Maybe Jones was right; they were going to find someone to blame this heinous crime on, close the case, and sweep everything under the rug. She looked at Lawson for an answer, but he adverted his eyes.

"We haven't had a hit on the drawing yet, but I'll look into it." Lawson explained.

"I think we have everything we need." Carson looked at Farren with cold hard eyes.

"That's it? This is my third interview and that's all you asked me?" She looked between the two detectives.

"Listen, we got most of the questions out of the way before." Carson voice was sharp and filled with anger.

"Ms. Bell, this follow-up is just to make sure we got everything we need. We don't want to miss anything." Lawson reassured her as he sent a narrowed eyed glare at his partner.

Farren nodded with a slight frown. She guessed this was their version of *good cop versus bad cop. However, she wasn't certain why they were playing the game with her.*

She still couldn't believe a couple of indirect questions and half ass reassurances was it. Carson was leading the case, and he didn't even look like he cared one way or another. These two would never find the killer.

Farren shook her head. It had already been over two months since she lived in her own house. She had changed her entire way of living because of what she saw. Now, at least she knew that she didn't do it for nothing since it was obvious that somebody was actually looking for her.

As soon as they exited the vehicle, Benny went directly to the security desk while Farren and Jones were met by the apartment manager in the lobby. Farren didn't live in a penthouse apartment, but her building was nice. You needed to be buzzed into the building, and there were camera's in the lobby and in the elevators. Farren always had a sense of security.

Mr. Brown was the apartment manager. He was a portly man with light brown skin and cloudy brown eyes. He was in his mid to late sixties and was the worst gossip that Farren knew. He was a very nice man though, and he always watched out for the tenants in the building.

"Oh, Farren! I was so worried that you were home, sweetheart. I'm so glad you're safe." Mr. Brown hugged Farren tightly, and Farren took comfort in the older man's embrace.

"Thank you, Mr. Brown. Do you have any idea when this happened?" Farren questioned.

"Well, the new guy in 4A said that he thought he heard something around midnight, but we didn't discover your door was open until this morning when Mrs. Dubinsky was walking Coco."

Farren sighed. She never thought she would be happy that nosy Mrs. Dubinsky used her dog to snoop, but in this case, she'd give the older woman a pass. But there was no telling who had been in her home, or how long they were there. It creeped her out.

"When were the police called?" Jones asked in his abrupt way of his.

"And just who are you, young man?" Mr. Brown glared at Jones, and Farren couldn't help but snicker.

"I'm Farren's boyfriend. When were the police called?" Jones asked again.

It was as if time had slowed down. Farren could see the shocked expression come over Mr. Brown's wrinkled features, and her face would've mirrored his, but she controlled her expressions. She turned her head slowly to look at Jones. His face was stone, but his eyes were a blazing green and gold fire. Farren knew then that it wasn't the time to address his comment, he was pissed that her house was broken into.

"Mr. Brown, are the police still here?"

Mr. Brown held his glare toward Jones a little longer before answering Farren. "Yes, they are still 'processing the scene' or whatever." Mr. Brown rolled his eyes.

Farren, Jones, and Benny were led to the elevator by Mr. Brown who followed them up to her apartment. Once they reached her door, there were only a couple of police officers there.

An Officer Miller asked Farren a couple of questions, and told her they couldn't tell if it was a burglary or not until she let them know if she was missing anything.

Mr. Brown had grossly misconstrued the state of her apartment. Although it was clear someone was looking for something, it wasn't exactly "trashed."

Drawers from every room were emptied onto the floor, papers were everywhere, and the couch was overturned. The TV was still mounted on the wall, her expensive DJing equipment was still in place, her gaming systems were still on the shelf, and her Alexa was still where she left it. As far as she could tell, this wasn't a robbery.

But what the hell were they looking for?

After checking her room and her jewelry box, Farren was able to let the officers know that she didn't think anything was missing. Officer Miller told her the report would be filed as a break-in but not a burglary.

Farren thanked the officers and after some rather invasive questions from Jones, the officers finally left.

"Obviously somebody was looking for something, but what?" Farren questioned both Jones and Benny.

"They were probably looking for information about you, kiddo," Benny replied, his eyes softening.

Farren saw Jones' mouth tighten into a thin line at Benny's affection, but she was too focused on what Benny said.

"This *has* to do with the case. Somebody got my information from the Titanic, and now the killer knows who I am. Shit!" Farren was frantic. She was certain that the cops weren't even looking for the pale-eyed killer, and asking them for help would've been pointless.

"How the hell did someone get your info from the Titanic? I'm so lost," Benny replied his handsome face lined in confusion.

"The Titanic... Dallas Metro PD," Jones answered.

"Oh, *that* Titanic." Benny nodded. "Yeah, that's exactly where they got your information."

"I'm sorry, sweetheart." Jones gathered Farren up in a comforting hug. "We can get someone in here to clean this mess up, but in the meantime, you need to pack a bag. There's no way you can live here until we figure out what's going on."

Farren was disappointed that she would have to continue staying with Eden, and not in the comfort of her own home. However, she realized the severity of the situation. Someone was in her home looking for something. And if she would've been there, she probably wouldn't have lived to tell about it.

"I'll go pack a bag, and call E. She'll need to know that her and Cam will have a house guest for an unknown amount of time," Farren stated absently as she headed toward her room.

———

Farren was lost in her own thoughts as she packed her large suitcase. It was as if she were having an out of body experience. She felt like she watched from the sidelines as her life spun out of her control. One night, and a poor decision to not walk the long way changed everything.

She didn't want to seem selfish. After all, a man did lose his life. But it was as if she was the only one that cared about that. Farren wanted the murder behind bars because he took a life without a second thought, and now he could very well be after her.

"Farren, you okay in here?" Jones questioned as he walked into her bedroom.

"Yeah, just thinking. I'm ready to get out of here." Farren went to grab her suitcase, but with one stern look, Jones stopped her.

"You know I got this," he said in warning.

Farren put her hands up in a surrendering motion.

"Did you call Eden yet?" Jones asked as he moved the suitcase by the door and sauntered to the bed to sit down beside her.

"Not yet. I wanted to pack first." The heavy sigh that left Farren didn't release any of the anxiety she was feeling.

"You know you could always stay with me." The look on Jones' handsome face was almost enough to make Farren consider his offer. But he was doing quite enough for her already without her intruding in on his home.

"Thank you, Jones. But I don't think that would be a good idea."

"Why not? I mean listen, you need a place to stay, and I want you with me. I don't see what the problem is."

"The problem is that now we're sleeping together. It would just complicate things if I'm living with you." Farren wanted him to understand where she was coming from. She didn't want to add onto an already stressful situation.

Jones ran his hand through his auburn hair. Farren could tell that he was frustrated, but she wasn't backing down from her decision. He was already doing so much for her, the last thing she wanted to do was impose on his space.

"Sweetheart, I really wish you'd reconsider." Farren could see that Jones meant what he said, but she would stick to her decision and stay with Eden.

"I really do appreciate the offer, Jones. Believe me you've done so much for me, but I'll be fine at Eden's."

He nodded his head in resignation, but Farren could tell by the stubborn glint in his eyes that this conversation wasn't over.

———

MURDERER

"Detective, I told you to have someone find information on the witness. Why did I get word that her apartment was broken into and trashed?" the pale eyed man questioned.

"My informant couldn't find what we asked him to, so he ransacked the place to make it look less suspicious."

"Less suspicious? He didn't take anything, so what he made it look like was exactly what it was... somebody looking for information. She's already got a bodyguard, so what do you think will happen with this little break-in?"

"Sir, I made a mistake," the detective responded.

"You're damn right. And you need to fucking fix it! I need a conviction of your suspect like yesterday. Are we understood?"

"Yes, sir. Underst..." The pale eyed man hung up before the bumbling idiot could finish his groveling. If he had to get involved in silencing this witness, it was not going to be pretty.

Chapter Seventeen

JONES

Jones had secured Farren at Eden's penthouse, and his disappointment was evident on his face as he headed home. He understood where Farren was coming from, and why she felt the need to stay with her friend instead of him. But spending more time together would only help them get to know one another better. He felt like they had taken ten steps forward and fifty steps back with her decision.

Of course things had changed between them, however. Having a sexual relationship was supposed to bring them closer not put a wedge between them. Then on top of everything, the Peter Ryan case was at a standstill, and he still hadn't gotten any news on the killer.

On top of all of the shit going on in his personal life, he was behind on some of his work responsibilities. Because Cam had taken up all the slack in his absence, Jones had to wine and dine the Simon Group at a charity event while Cam schmoozed and relaxed. But that was the penance Jones had to pay.

He decided that he would try and get caught up on some paperwork for some of his properties. Jones had several properties in North Texas that he and Camedon had invested in. They were in the middle of a huge commercial remodel, and Jones needed to make sure everything stayed on track with the contractors.

Jones was in deep concentration when his cell phone vibrated with a new voicemail. He was so into the contract he hadn't heard his phone buzz. He listened to the message that his old friend left him, and he was so relieved that they finally had a suspect for the Ryan case.

The perp had ties to Peter Ryan, had pale blue eyes, and a record a mile long. Linda was pretty certain that they had the right guy. Two more witnesses had come forward and picked the guy out of a line-up, so the detectives working the case were gathering evidence against the man.

It felt like a weight was instantly lifted off of Jones' shoulders with the news. He couldn't wait to tell Farren. He wondered if the detectives had called her to make an ID. Jones really hoped that she wouldn't have gone to the police station without telling him, but Farren was unpredictable when it came to relying on someone else. *Or maybe it was just relying on me.*

Jones decided he wouldn't put off calling Farren because he would never be able to concentrate on work until he spoke with her.

Her cell rang twice before her husky voice vibrated through the line.

"Hey, Sugar. You doin' okay?"

"Umm... so I'm 'Sugar' today, huh?" Farren questioned with a throaty chuckle.

"Yeah, well you're the sweetest thing I've ever tasted, so yeah... Sugar seems appropriate." Jones couldn't help the smile that broke out on his face. There was just something about Farren Bell that had him feeling like a teenager again.

"Uh huh... why are you trying to charm me Jones Sullivan?" Jones had a feeling that Farren was smiling and he was also pretty sure that she was blushing.

"I can't help the charm, Sugar, it's just who I am." Jones arrogantly chuckled.

Farren laughed. "Okay 'Charming' what's up? You just left me a couple of hours ago."

"I got some news on the case," Jones replied. His voice turned serious. "I was just checking to see if the detectives had notified you yet."

"No, no one has called me." Jones heard the slight tremble in Farren's voice. "What happened?"

Jones proceeded to tell Farren all the information Officer Michaels told him, and he could hear the relief in her voice loud and clear. He was ecstatic that he was the person to bring her a sense of peace. Now maybe things could get back to normal, and he could start back to actively pursuing his obsession without distraction.

———

It had been a couple of days since Jones had gotten news of the killer's identity, and after his own investigating, some things for him just weren't adding up. However, Farren felt more comfortable and had even made plans to move back into her apartment at the end of the week. Jones didn't want to rain on her parade, so he kept his suspicions to himself for now.

Jones put all of his efforts into his work, the charity event for the Simon group was tonight, and he had a lot of preparations to do for the annual Euphoria masquerade event coming up. He wanted to take Farren to both events, but he'd only asked her to the charity event.

It had only been a week since they had been to Euphoria, and although things had calmed down with the suspect being named, both he and Farren had been busy with work, and hadn't been able to see much of each other. Tonight, they would make up for lost time.

Jones was excited to get the chance to take Farren out to the event, but most importantly, he couldn't wait to bring her home and ravish her glorious bountiful body.

Jones was dressed in his slim fit black tuxedo with matching black tie. The dark silver vest contrasted nicely against the stark white dress shirt, and his coppery skin tone. His five o'clock shadow was trimmed and lined with his perfectly styled hair. Jones looked dangerously handsome and he knew it.

Benny drove him to pick-up Farren, and when she walked into Camedon's living room from the guest room, he couldn't help the wide-eyed stare he gave her. She was wearing a trumpet style dress with spaghetti straps. The dress had a v-neckline and bodice. It looked like someone had poured liquid silver over her voluptuous curves. Jones thought he was going to lose his mind, but when she did a little twirl to show him the entire dress, he almost had a heart attack. The back had the same v-design as the front except it dipped dangerously low. The dress fit her body perfectly. Farren was all woman and he loved that about her.

"So what do you think?" Farren asked with a heated glint in her eyes as she took him in.

"Farren, you look absolutely gorgeous. I can't wait to get you out of that dress." Jones smiled wickedly. There were so many things he wanted to do to her at that very moment, but he would hold it together long enough for them to go to the event and have a good time.

"Thank you." Farren's face flushed slightly. "Now may I tell you that you look good enough to eat, Sugar." Farren tried to mock his voice, and Jones laughed loudly.

"Was that supposed to be me?" He continued to laugh at her silliness.

"Of course it was you. Who else would it be?" She laughed.

Jones pulled Farren into his arms, cuddled her close, and rained kisses on her neck. "Well, Sugar, I'm pretty sure you're way tastier than I'll ever be. Now let's get going, so I can get you back home to devour you."

Chapter Eighteen

FARREN

The ride to the event was full of heated glances, and even hotter words. Farren was ready to peel herself out of her dress and hump him in the back of his SUV... again. She just couldn't get over how he brought out this lusty side to her.

He looked so damn good in his tuxedo. The fabric fit his lean muscled form perfectly. His hair was gelled, with a side part, the top styled away from his face.

He looks like a white Jidenna, but way sexier, Farren thought with a smile. *Now I'm going to be singing "Classic Man" for the rest of the night.* She smirked at her thoughts.

"What are you over there smirking about?" Jones asked with a voice laced with curiosity.

"Oh, just thinking about how *classically* handsome you are. Red." Farren smiled devilishly at her own inside joke.

He smirked back at her. "I *don't* look like Jidenna. And my hair is NOT red, but us *auburn* haired fellas do have to stick together." He winked at her with a crooked smile spreading across his chiseled face.

"What do you know about Jidenna?" Farren laughed.

"First of all, like I said, all of us auburn haired men have to stick together, and secondly, you've played him on your radio show, so I know who he is." Jones smiled, his eyes twinkling with something Farren couldn't decipher.

Farren turned away from the look in his eyes to gather her thoughts before changing the subject. "So what's with the 'auburn'? You know you're a ginger, right?"

"My hair is *not* red," Jones stated again. His face held a scowl but the laughter dancing in his eyes gave him away.

"Umkay. 'Red', whatever you say, sir." Farren giggled, but the laughter was cut short by the seductive look on Jones' face.

"If sir is something you want to call me officially, we can definitely make that happen." Jones quirked a brow at her.

Farren smiled in response, but mumbled "freak" under her breath. There was no way she was going to walk into that conversation willingly... at least, not right now.

Benny pulled the SUV in front of an architectural masterpiece. Farren had heard great things about this new museum, but she had never been before. The beauty of the building was breathtaking. The sharp angles, exposed metal beams, and modern design had Farren instantly intrigued about the inside of the place.

"I'm not going to valet. I'll park and be along in a minute," Benny stated after opening Farren's door. Jones nodded, and led them down a red carpet.

"I didn't realize there was going to be a red carpet." Farren was wowed by all of the hoopla surrounding the event.

"You know we like to go all out around here." Jones smiled.

"Well, that's mighty bougie of you." Farren smiled back.

Jones laughed loudly as they stopped and posed for pictures.

Farren had been to plenty of red carpet events. However, she was usually working them, interviewing celebrities for her show, or her fashion blog. But she had never been on this side of the carpet before, Farren felt unquestionably glamorous.

———

The event was in full swing, and it was quite the swanky affair. Even the mayor was present. Farren was glad that they had a suspect in custody, so maybe Mayor Ryan could get some closure for his nephew. The detectives on the case had called to schedule her to come in for an identification, but at this point, it was just a formality since there were two other witness' that had made a positive identification. Farren smiled politely to the other guests that were milling around the event. She had to stop her dark thoughts, so she decided to get a drink.

Jones was off taking an important phone call, so Farren decided to keep herself busy. She perused the items for the silent auction while she sipped her glass of champagne. She was surprised that the Simon Group was putting on a charity event to raise money for the Children's Hospital of North Texas. Although the men she met from the organization seemed like nice guys, they didn't really strike her as the philanthropic type.

Farren spotted an item she wanted to bid on, so she made her way over to the elaborately decorated table. The item for auction was a weekend spa getaway package. She decided to bid high. It was for a good cause after all.

Farren was finishing chatting with the attendant at the spa table when she felt someone's finger trace her spine. She knew it wasn't Jones because the touch and feel of the finger was all wrong. Under normal circumstances, she would have acted a damn fool, and throat punched the hell out of somebody. However, since she was in her Sunday best, and here with all these fancy people representing with Jones, Farren decided to act more dignified.

She twirled around with her eye's narrowed on the culprit. "Excuse you. Is there a reason you felt comfortable enough to touch me? Do I know you?" Farren asked through clenched teeth to the man with dark wicked eyes that she remembered from Euphoria. She didn't remember his name but the creepy feeling she remembered he gave her was back in full force.

He smiled a creepy smile like she was standing in front of him completely naked. "Of course you know me. Alexander Parsons. Remember, we met a few days ago. I just wanted to come and say hello."

"You did more than say hello. It would be best for your health if you kept your hands to yourself." Farren's tone was calm but the fire in her eyes showed her displeasure.

"I apologize. I didn't mean to offend you." To Farren's dismay, his smile got creepier.

"Hmmm." Farren gave a noncommittal nod and looked away.

"You looked so delicious... in your dress. I just couldn't help myself." He moved in closer, invading her personal space.

Farren took a step back, putting space between her and Parsons. There was something about this man she didn't like, and the fact that he was blatantly hitting on her when he knew she was with Jones was grossly inappropriate and rude as hell.

The last thing Farren wanted to do was have an awkward conversation with this creepy ass man, and it was not something that she was about to do.

"Excuse me, I need to..." Farren couldn't even come up with a good excuse. She didn't want to seem rude, but *fuck it*. Farren walked away without finishing her sentence.

It was clear that boundaries and respect weren't things the man knew much about, and it wasn't her job to teach him.

Farren walked quickly to the other side of the room when she noticed her saving grace standing at a table that was auctioning off services of a well renowned chef.

"Elyse, what are you doing here?" Farren asked her friend, relieved that she knew someone besides Jones and Benny.

"Hey, Farren!" Elyse replied hugging Farren. "I'm here to support daddy. You know he's on the board for the Children's Hospital."

"Right, of course. Then where is your sister?"

"She's here somewhere, schmoozing with Cam I'm sure," Elyse replied with a smile.

"I thought Cam wasn't coming? When Jones and I were on the way here..."

"Hold the hell up..." Elyse interrupted before Farren could finish her sentence. "Jones, as in Sullivan? You and Jones came here... together." Elyse was acting like she just got the hottest tea she had ever tasted.

Farren forgot that Elyse hadn't been around lately, which was something Farren had to ask her about, so she didn't know about her and Jones.

"Yes," she answered simply.

"Oh ho ho." Elyse laughed knowingly. "So you finally got that ass on the swirl train huh?" She smiled wickedly.

Farren could only laugh at Elyse's silliness. "Girl, I'm not only on the train, I'm the damn conductor." Both ladies laughed loudly until they noticed the curious gazes of the other guests and they stifled their laughter.

"Well it's about damn time. So how was it?" Elyse moved her eyebrows up and down suggestively.

"Uh, no ma'am, this is neither the time or the place for this conversation. So get yo mind out tha gutta." Farren laughed again.

"Girl please, my mind has a permanent residence in tha gutta." Elyse laughed as well.

Elyse and Farren talked and laughed as they moved around the event. Jones still hadn't made it back yet, and Farren started to wonder where he went. Just when she was about to excuse herself, a tall, handsome brown-skinned man with striking green eyes approached them.

Damn! He's fine as hell! Farren looked at Elyse to see if she was looking at the same jade-eyed tall glass of chocolate milk headed their way, and Elyse definitely saw him if the look on her face was any indication.

"Hello ladies." The man's voice was like melted caramel, smooth and decadent.

"Hello." They both replied breathlessly in unison.

"I'm Travis Stanley. I wanted to come introduce myself to you all. I couldn't help but notice that you were bidding on our silent auction, and I wanted to thank you for your participation in tonight's events."

"Nice to meet you." Farren shook the man's hand.

"It's nice to meet you Mr. Stanley. I'm Elyse." Elyse smiled widely as the handsome man took her hand in his and shook.

He held Elyse's hand a little longer than necessary, and Farren felt like she was intruding on an intimate moment between the two. She cleared her throat loudly to draw Elyse's attention. Elyse was slow to break eye contact with the attractive stranger, but when she looked at

Farren with a "heffa you're interrupting my game" look, Farren chuckled and stepped back, giving the couple room to flirt.

"Call me Travis, please," Farren heard the man say as she turned away from their conversation.

When the intensity of their flirting picked up, Farren excused herself to the ladies' room. She wasn't sure what was going on with Elyse and Harper, but by Elyse's behavior towards Travis, maybe her budding romance with Harper had died off.

Farren shrugged at the thought. It wasn't her business, and she wouldn't get involved in other people's relationships. She had her own to figure out.

As she sauntered across the packed space, she could feel the wanton gazes of some of the men in the room. Farren didn't hate the heated stares, or the attention. She wasn't vain or starved for admiration, but with all the effort she put into her outfit tonight, she was happy that she was being noticed.

Farren admired the pieces of modern art as she made her way upstairs to the restroom. The art was unique and vibrant in an array of colors, the contrast to the stark white walls and metal beams was truly a sight to behold.

It had been thirty minutes since Jones had received his call, and not for the first time since he stepped away she began to wonder where he was.

"I could just watch you all night." The deep voice gave her chills, and she couldn't help the slow smile that spread across her face as strong arms wrapped around her from behind.

Chapter Nineteen

JONES

He had spent the last thirty minutes dealing with a small electrical fire at one of his construction sites. The fire didn't get out of hand, and the night guard on the property was able to put it out and call for help. Jones spent his time calling in favors for an electrician to go by the site and take a precautionary look at everything. It was going to cost an arm and a leg, but he found someone to do the job.

Jones came back into the venue in search of his beautiful date. He saw her from across the room as she chatted with Elyse and some fucker that was standing too close for his liking. Jones was about to make his way over, but he saw Farren walk away.

Instead of making himself known, he followed and watched her with interest. Her face lit up as she took in the beautiful art. Farren's dressed flowed seamlessly around her body making her even more beautiful than the art she was admiring. Jones was aware of all the men, and some women, that were openly ogling his date.

Jones learned to share as a kid, he did have six brothers after all, so being stingy had never been an issue for him. Even as an adult, he wasn't averse to sharing. However, to watch as multiple men devoured Farren with their lustful eyes made even the thought of sharing something he despised.

Jones felt like a stalker again as he watched her not making her aware of his presence. But he couldn't help himself. Farren always brought out the voyeur side in him.

"I could just watch you all night."

"Why just watch when you can touch," came Farren's sassy retort.

Jones pulled her soft body against his as he wrapped his arms around her from behind. His hands moved down the front of her dress. He had the overwhelming need to touch her, and he relished in the feeling of his hands on her body.

"You look good enough to eat..." Jones nipped at her neck, and she moved her head to the side to give him more room.

Jones loved that she wasn't a woman that shied away from what she wanted. *My match, h*e thought as he continued to caress her neck with feather light kisses.

"Mmmm." Farren moaned and the sound made his erection grow.

"Come with me," he commanded. Jones pulled Farren into an unoccupied restroom and locked the door.

Jones had a decision to make. Either he tore the dress from her body like a crazy person, or found some way underneath it. He rubbed his chin contemplating which would be more fun.

"Don't you even think about it, Jones Sullivan."

"What?" He made his eyes go wide with what he hoped conveyed his innocence, but the no-nonsense look that marred Farren's pretty round face told him he failed miserably.

"Don't 'what' me. You already owe me one outfit." She placed her hands on her curvy hips. "This is a dignified event, and I won't leave here draped in your jacket because you tore up my dress." Farren's eyebrow arched in challenge.

Jones held up his hands in surrender. "Okay, but I'm not going to last all night with you sashaying your pretty ass around in that dress. So I'm going to need a little taste to help me make it."

"A little taste, huh?" The mirth in Farren's eyes turned to unadulterated want, and Jones knew that he had her.

"Yes, just a little." Jones held his thumb and finger up to indicate how much. "I mean, come on Sugar, you can't possibly think a man like me could ever resist you. Hell, any man for that matter. Especially dipped in silver, smelling so sweet."

"Uh huh." Farren replied but he knew he had her.

"Why don't I help you have a seat, I'm sure your feet are killing you in those shoes." He picked Farren up easily and placed her on a thick modern vanity table that was against the wall.

With a gasp she held on as he pushed her long gown up around her thighs. He spread her legs apart and went to his knees. Jones worked the dress up to give him more room, and he was thankful that Farren was a girl of habit. *No panties.*

Jones licked his lips; the smell of her arousal overwhelmed his senses. Her scent intoxicated him, and he dove in head first. He kissed her lower lips sensually. His tongue delved between her sugary folds as he tasted her honeyed essence. Farren moaned and squirmed, but Jones held her thighs tightly to make sure she couldn't move.

Jones added a finger and when her breathed hitched on a low moan, he knew that he had hit her spot. He sucked on her clit, adding pressure with his tongue, as his finger rubbed her g-spot over and over again.

"I'm coming baby, please don't stop." Farren groaned breathlessly. She worked her hips erotically while Jones continued to thrust his finger into her warm wet cove.

Jones didn't stop. He hummed, knowing that the vibrations would send her over the cliff. And they did.

Farren's moans grew louder, so Jones quickly rose to his feet and took her lips in a kiss to quiet her. He kept his finger moving, and he could feel her pussy clench around his probing digit. Farren's breathing slowly settled, and Jones finally pulled his finger from her channel. He slipped his finger into his mouth and moaned his delight. Jones knew that Farren liked his erotic display, and it was becoming somewhat of a ritual to taste her in this way. Her face was flushed, and her fiery eyes watched his tongue swirl around his finger.

The heat in the depths of her eyes had his dick pulsating with want, but he would wait to get her home. He promised he just wanted a taste, so he would delay the inevitable for just a little while longer.

I can wait. Jones ran his hand through his hair as he tried to calm down. He took a deep breath, took his handkerchief out of his pocket, and cleaned her essence from her thighs with it, he helped Farren off the table, and straightened her dress.

Farren gave him a shy smile and a kiss before her hand slipped into her small clutch purse. She slipped a piece of gum in her mouth and handed him one.

"You're gonna need this." She winked. Jones smirked as he cleaned his face and popped the gum in his mouth.

———

The hunger that Jones felt for Farren only intensified after their little bathroom tryst. She was so vibrant and approachable, everyone seemed to flock to her. Her laughter carried throughout the space and everyone around her seemed to smile at the sound.

Jones knew that he and Farren were just embarking on this new part of their relationship, but he had the overwhelming need to be with her every minute that he could. She was a breath of fresh air in what had become his mundane life.

They were mingling with the other guests after dinner as they waited on the silent auction results to be announced when Jones saw Benny motion for him. Jones excused himself from Farren and the group to see what was up with his friend and head of security.

"We have a major problem," Benny stated without preamble, his chocolate face lined with seriousness.

Jones nodded for Benny to continue, but his senses were now on high alert.

"The mayor is here. He's supposed to make the announcements about the auction."

Jones didn't know why that would be a problem, but he let Benny continue without interrupting him.

"For an event like this, most of the big wigs have security. I was in the security office, and I saw someone interesting on the video feed speaking with the mayor."

Benny handed Jones his phone with a recording of the live feed from the office. When Jones saw the pale eyed bastard he instantly knew that Dallas Metro was full of shit because the man they had in custody wasn't the killer. Because the man Farren saw kill Peter Ryan was talking to the mayor.

Chapter Twenty

FARREN

Farren had an absolute blast at the charity event. She was so anxious about going at first. This wasn't the first charity event that she'd been to, but she'd always gone with friends, or at least she would know people there. Farren was also apprehensive about people from Euphoria being there. Farren had never been to Euphoria without a mask until the week before, so she didn't know what to expect if people recognized her or how they would behave knowing she was a part of a taboo lifestyle.

Farren wasn't at all embarrassed by her involvement at Euphoria or the lifestyle she chose to lead. She was a grown ass woman, and her choices were hers to make. She didn't expect anyone else to live her way, but previously she had always worn a mask while partaking in club activities. The last time she was without a mask, so people recognizing her and her recognizing them was new for her.

As it turned out, most everyone was very cordial and even down-right friendly; except for Alexander Parsons. His actions proved what a douche he indeed was, and exactly what he thought of Farren. He treated her as if she were a piece of meat to be consumed at his will. However, she wouldn't let one asshole ruin her good time, so she didn't.

And on top of everything, all of her worrying about not knowing anyone was for nothing anyway since Elyse and Eden showed up. Farren had no idea that they were even going to be there because she had been so wrapped up with working at the station, her fashion blog, and worrying about the murder investigation that she didn't even mention that she was going to the event.

Farren was so busy thinking about the events of the night that she almost didn't notice how quiet Jones was. Normally if they didn't have some heated exchange or witty banter between the two of them, their silence was comfortable. But Farren noticed that at the moment, there was a tension in the air that wasn't normally there.

Jones was staring out of the window, his fist clenching and unclenching, as his leg bounced up and down. Farren had never seen Jones display any of those nervous behaviors before, and she instantly frowned.

He was clearly upset about something, but she couldn't think of anything that happened that would cause him to act so distant, and upset.

"Hey there, Sugar... penny for your thoughts." Farren tried to mimic Jones' voice while she rubbed her hand up and down his bouncing knee.

He let out a small chuckle. "Your impression of me stinks, Sugar."

Farren shrugged, "not the point. You're talking to me instead of brooding in silence, so my impression worked."

Jones' face broke out into a mischievous grin, and Farren knew that her plan to lighten the mood worked.

"So what's on your mind, sunshine?" Farren asked again.

"Just work, baby, nothing important. I promise." Jones' face turned serious again as he kissed her hand and pulled her closer to his warmth.

Farren had a feeling that he was hiding something, but if he promised it was nothing, she would let it go... for now.

———

"I hope it's okay if we stay at my house tonight," Jones stated with a look of worry etched on his handsome face. Farren was so deep in thought that once again she failed to realize that the car had stopped.

When she took in Jones' facial expression, she decided that she wouldn't press him on what was going on with him. Farren instead decided to try to keep the mood light and give him less to think about.

"Yeah, that's fine. Are you going to buy me clothes again for tomorrow?" she asked cheekily with a playful smile.

Jones smiled in that devilishly charming way of his and replied, "I'll buy you anything you want, Sugar."

Farren couldn't resist his sexy mouth any longer, so she kissed him softly and then bit into his soft pink bottom lip until she heard him growl.

When she leaned back to look him in his glowing hazel eyes, she couldn't help the shiver that ran up her spine.

I'm about to get it! She smiled wickedly.

As usual, Jones led Farren through his lobby gripping her hand tightly. Farren wasn't especially big on holding hands, but with Jones it was just a natural occurrence. She wanted to be close to him at all times, and the connection she felt between them was strong.

There was still a tension in the air, and Farren couldn't put her finger on why that was, but the intensity fueled their love making, and it was out of this world. There weren't any dirty words, or ripping of clothes, just a slow methodical connection between the two of them.

The meticulous reverence he paid to her body overwhelmed Farren's senses. Her body felt a heat like never before. Jones worshiped every dip and curve to Farren's voluptuous physique, and she couldn't get enough.

The slow loving way he pushed into her warm core made the connection even stronger than it had ever been between them. Farren felt the change in their relationship as it happened, and without words she showed Jones with her body that she wholeheartedly accepted it.

MURDERER

"The suspect we questioned has an alibi. We're not going to be able to hold him, even with the witness identifications."

"So what you're telling me is... you're incompetent, and I have to do your job for you. That's what you're telling me, correct?" The pale-eyed man questioned the detective.

"No, sir. We had to find someone with specific characteristics that matched the initial witness statements. He was the best candidate under the circumstances," the detective tried to explain.

"Well obviously if he has a damn alibi then he wasn't the best fucking person!" The man's voice raised to a roar.

"Sir, we..."

"Your services are no longer needed. I'll handle this shit myself," the man interrupted.

"Sir, I can do the job," the detective tried again.

"If you could do the job, it would've been done by now. Goodbye Detective Lawson." The man hung up without another word.

As soon as he disconnected the call, the man made another one. "I need to speak to Mayor Ryan. This is Tobin Hunter, his head of security."

Chapter Twenty-One

JONES

Jones was fighting mad after he saw the video of the murderer talking to the mayor. The fact that a scumbag like him was right under their noses, and in the same vicinity as Farren made him want to do bodily harm to someone.

Jones had Benny working overtime trying to find out who the man was, but nobody recognized him, and nobody knew his name. It was as if he didn't exist.

It had been over a week since the charity event, and he was getting nowhere. Jones' frustration level was through the roof, and he knew that he was going to have to call in the big guns.

The phone rang twice before the deep voice answered, "Hey, little brother. What a surprise. You must be in deep shit to call me."

"Jax, I need your help," Jones stated seriously.

The mirth left his brother's voice instantly. "Who do I need to kill?"

"Not over the phone. Meet me in fifteen minutes at my office." Jones wanted to make sure they were in a safe place to talk freely. The offices of Price and Sullivan was the most secure place he owned. After Cam's crazy assistant Sam was able to break in with a gun, they made sure that the security there was top notch.

If Jones and Jax had to discuss some improper methods of getting a murderer off the streets, then they would be safe to do so.

Jones' older brother Jax was the one person that could give him the help that he needed to find out who the man with the pale blue eyes was. Jax was the brother they referred to as "Ghost." He was always there when you needed him, but you never really knew where he was going or where he'd been.

Jones was one of the only people that knew what Jax's actual job was, but he would never tell a soul. His brother did very dangerous things, but he was the only person he knew that would be able to solve the mystery surrounding what Farren had seen.

Jones didn't want to get his brother involved in his mess because he didn't want to risk his safety, but he was left with no other choice once he found out that the police had the wrong man in custody. It was imperative to keep Farren safe, and he would do that any way that he could.

In less than fifteen minutes, Jax walked into Jones' office. His brother stood at the same height of six foot four, his hazel eyes were more green than golden brown like Jones' were, but they could've still passed for twins if it weren't for Jax's light brown hair.

"I need to know why you waited until the last minute to call me?" Jax asked without any preamble as he sat down in the leather chair across from Jones' desk.

"How do you know I waited until the last minute? I haven't even told you what I needed from you yet," Jones stated with his arms crossed over his broad chest.

"I know you, little brother. You always want to do everything yourself. I told you the last time you had an issue, family comes first. You should've called me sooner."

Jones nodded. "You're right."

Even though he shouldn't have been, Jones was flabbergasted at his brother's accurate perception. He and Jax were always like two peas in a pod, and his brother knew him well even now.

Jones spent about an hour telling Jax every detail about the case and Farren. He showed him copies of the sketch of the killer Farren described as well as the recent video of the man talking to the mayor.

"This guy... I don't know him, but he seems familiar to me some-how," Jax stated as he stared at the picture like he was trying to solve a puzzle.

"That's weird. When I first saw him, I had the same feeling. He had a face that I felt like I'd seen but I couldn't place him for some reason."

Jax's head nodded in agreement. Jones watched closely as his broth-er's eyes meticulously scanned the information, and Jones knew that he wasn't in this alone, his brother was invested, and they were going to find this son of a bitch and make him pay.

Finally, Jax looked up from the information. "Somebody is helping this guy. There are very few people who can up and disappear unless..."

"Unless they're like you..." Jones finished his brother's statement.

Jax sighed heavily and sat back in his seat, "If this guy is a merce-nary, I'm going to have to call in some favors. And I hate to say this but..."

"Farren is in deeper shit than we thought..." Jones finished again. *Shit!*

———

Jax left Jones' office after another hour of discussing possible solutions. They came up empty at every turn, and both brothers were extremely frustrated. Jax had called in some old contacts in his underground network, and he was waiting for call backs. There would definitely be some information coming, but how long it would take was the prob-lem. Jax's contacts were spread out all over the world doing various things, so it could be a couple of hours up to a couple of months before they heard anything.

Jones felt better for having his brother on the case, but he defi-nitely wanted to get this shit resolved asap.

Jones tried to reset and get his mind on the operations of his busi-nesses. The Euphoria annual masquerade ball was coming up, and this year it was bigger than it had ever been before. With all of the new investment deals Price and Sullivan corporation had, they had more exclusive clients and more members of the club than ever. The converted warehouse space they rented for the party was being transformed into their version of Earth, Heaven, and Hell. Of course Jones' mask would contain devilish designs.

Previously, Jones would go simple with a plain black mask because he didn't have anyone to impress. His mind was always on how to get a beautiful woman or women into his bed. However, this year would be different. He had someone to impress, and he was going to do just that.

Farren should be on a pedestal, and with all of the shit she was going through, she earned the right more than anything to have some fun. Jones was going to do everything in his power to make sure she wasn't worried about the sick fuck that killed Peter Ryan. He would worry enough for the both of them, but in the meantime, he would distract her as best he could. And what was a better distraction than a beautiful erotic party full of sex...

Chapter Twenty-Two

FARREN

Ever since the night of the charity event, Jones had been distant. Although they saw each other often, and talked a lot, he always seemed preoccupied. Farren wanted to give Jones the benefit of the doubt, and she hoped with all of her heart he wasn't one of those men that chased until he captured and then the game was over.

Jones had a reputation for loving and leaving the women he was involved with, and she thought that she was different... *but maybe I'm not.*

Farren wasn't one of those insecure women that questioned everything about her relationships, but everything about her and Jones was different.

Maybe I will just ask him what's wrong.

Her cell phone ringing brought her out of her thoughts. It was an unlisted number which she usually wouldn't answer, but it could've been the detectives calling for a follow-up.

"Hello?" Farren answered her voice laced with caution.

"Hey, Farren, it's Mr. Brown. I was just calling to let you know that the cleaning service you hired just left, so I went ahead and had the locks changed on your doors."

Farren was glad to hear from Mr. Brown. He had been keeping a close eye on her place since the break-in. Farren decided to take Jones' advice and hire a cleaning service to straighten up her place. Mr. Brown changing the locks helped Farren feel like her house was more secure.

"Thanks, Mr. Brown. You don't know how much I appreciate you."

"Oh, little girl, don't you worry yourself. You're like one of my grandbabies, I would help you any way that I could." Mr. Brown was a kind man and Farren was thankful for all of his help.

"You can come by and pick up your new keys whenever you're ready."

"Okay, great! I'll be by later. Thanks again, for everything."

They said their good-byes and Farren felt better about the situation already. She had to admit to herself that she needed a distraction from all the mess that was going on.

Farren had only posted on her *Curvy Girl Sway* Blog twice since the whole situation started. It had been three and half months and she was ready to get her life back.

The suspect for the murder was in custody, and although she hadn't found a new station to work at yet, Evan had been leaving her alone since she threatened to go to HR. She needed some normalcy back in her life, so maybe it was time she moved back into her apartment.

Benny could still drive her to and from work if necessary, and she could beef up her security system at her place. Farren also felt that Cam and Eden needed their space back and she was ready to be back in her own place.

It was time she took control over her own life. Farren decided that she would go pick up her keys, check on her place, and then come back and get ready for the masquerade ball. Jones asked her to accompany him, and even though he wasn't acting like his usual self, she would take advantage of the opportunity to have a little fun.

"B-nice, hey it's Farren. I just wanted to see if you were available, but since I got your voicemail it looks like you're busy. If you get this in the next few minutes give me a call." Farren hung up the phone and sighed.

"It looks like I'll have to put my big girl panties on, and do this

Leabharlanna Fhine Gall

myself," Farren mumbled to herself. She took a deep breath, and started packed some of her things. "It's time I get my life back!"

———

Thirty minutes later, Farren was pulling her car into her designated parking spot at her building. She noticed right away that there was a new security guard patrolling the lot, and she was glad that they were taking the break-in seriously by beefing up security.

Farren nodded at the man as she made her way inside to see Mr. Brown. It took her another twenty minutes of reassuring the caring older man that she was fine, and would be moving back in very soon.

After getting her new set of keys, she made her way to her apartment. Farren felt an odd sensation that someone was watching her. However, every time she looked around, there was nobody there.

I'm just being paranoid. Get it together, girl.

Farren boarded the elevator, and pushed the button for her floor. As the elevator doors closed, she made eye contact with the new security guard again. Farren meant to ask Mr. Brown about the man but she forgot.

Maybe on the way out, she thought as the elevator doors shut fully.

When Farren finally made it to her apartment, she thought she would feel unsafe or violated like the last time she was there. But there was no residual nervousness from the break in left. Farren let out a relieved breath.

Farren inspected her place making sure the cleaners did what they were supposed to do. They did a great job. Her apartment was spotless. *Maybe I will hire a cleaner more often.*

Farren spent most of the afternoon and some of the evening getting reacquainted with her home. She unpacked some of her things, and made herself comfortable. It was a good time to post on her blog, and put some more feelers out for another radio station.

Before she knew it, it was time for her to go back to Eden's and get ready for the masquerade ball. Farren decided that she would stick to the original plan of getting ready at Eden's because they were going to all ride to the venue together.

The sun had set and Farren decided she needed to head back to the penthouse to get ready. She was excited about the night and all of the festivities that she was sure to indulge in. Farren had never been to the Euphoria Masquerade Ball before, and excited was not a word to characterize the level of enthusiasm she felt.

When she told Eden that Jones had ask her to the party, the shock that registered on her best friend's face was comical. Farren also had to break down and tell her friend the truth about Euphoria.

"So you know Jones asked me to go to the masquerade ball." Farren said casually as she and Eden lounged around her living room.

Eden's head turned toward Farren in slow motion, and her wide eyes and opened mouth conveyed Eden's surprise.

"Wow, that's a huge step for you guys. I mean Euphoria is not your run-of-the-mill club. And from what I heard, the masquerade ball is something out of this world."

Farren nodded. Wondering just how her bestie was going to take the fact that she'd been to Euphoria and had been holding it a secret for several months already.

"Even Cam warned me about the debauchery that happens at the masquerade, and I practically live at Euphoria. I mean what did Jones tell you about the party?" Eden questioned her face was hesitant, but Farren could see that she was trying to be supportive.

Farren decided nonchalant would be the best way to break the news. "I'm sure it will be fine, anyway I've been to Euphoria several times, and I handled it just..."

"Hold the hell up," Eden interrupted putting her palm directly in Farren's face. "I know damn well you didn't just casually try to slip passed me that you've had your fass ass to Euphoria not once, but several times."

"Uh... well I didn't really know how to break it to you that Erick took me there. You didn't care for him, so I never brought it up." Farren answered sheepishly.

"Bihha, the hell! Do you really think I'm going to let you blame this on that bum, Erick?"

"I was hoping you would." Farren smiled trying to get Eden to calm down.

"No ma'am. Absolutely not! You had ample opportunity to tell me you'd been

to Euphoria. *All of the times I've given you the tea about my exploits and you had your own!"*

"I know... my bad E-boogie."

"*Oh no you don't, E-boogie me! You don't just owe me tea; you owe me a grand slam breakfast heffa.*" Eden's hand landed on her popped hip, and Farren knew by that little pose alone that she was forgiven. But she also knew that she would have to give up some juicy details of her shenanigans or it would be hell to pay.

"*I'm sorry bestie. I promise to give you all the tea your little heart desires.*"

"*You have no choice*" Eden replied sassily.

Farren was glad that the cat was finally out of the bag, and she no longer had to tiptoe around the subject of Euphoria. After it was all said and done, she wasn't sure why she kept it a secret for so long in the first place.

At first, it was because she didn't want to feel judged for her choice, but after Eden met Cam, that was no longer an excuse. But she continued to hold the secret, and now she felt foolish for not just coming out with the truth.

However, all that was behind her now. And tonight she could relax with Jones and hopefully have a delightfully naughty night.

Chapter Twenty-Three

JONES

Jones wanted to be excited about the masquerade ball, but his attention had been focused on finding the asshole murderer that was in cahoots with the fucking mayor of all people.

Jax's contacts had finally come through and they finally had a name, Tobin Hunter. He was a former mercenary, and a very bad man. He was suspected of numerous assassinations and murders. It was believed that Tobin Hunter wasn't even his real name, but a man like him had the skills to disappear and reinvent himself numerous times.

Jones had found the man responsible for such a heinous crime, but he needed proof. And he needed to find out what the mayor's involvement was. Was the mayor a victim, being blackmailed or threatened, or was he the reason his nephew was dead? Jones had too much shit to figure out. On top of all that, he had to keep Farren safe until he could get all this shit resolved. However, the masquerade ball was their biggest event of the year, so he had to suck it up, and get himself together.

Although they would be in a warehouse full of people wearing masks the extreme security measures they took would prevent anything from happening.

Also, the ball was invitation only, and the guest list was a closely guarded secret. Only a select few knew the names, and there was no way anyone could get into the venue if they weren't invited. The clientele were rich and powerful people, and their anonymity was important.

Jones was even more confident in their security because this year, like all of the previous years, there were no cell phones or electronic devices permitted. However, if someone decided to sneak something in, Camedon had an EMP or electromagnetic pulse device that was used to knock out electronic devices in its range on the property just for the masquerade.

The security had special transmitters that allowed them to communicate and hidden cameras that was on a separate network that surrounded the outside of the venue. Even with all the precautions that were taken, Jones knew that his guard would still be up and tonight would not be his usual erotic time at the masquerade.

Benny was on duty for the evening, and that made Jones feel better to have extra eyes and ears on the situation. He trusted Benny and he knew that he could count on him especially when it came to Farren's safety.

Jones looked at the time, and decided he should get ready for the night's festivities. Just because he wouldn't be relaxed completely, didn't mean he couldn't look like the debonair charmer that he was.

He dressed in black tuxedo pants with a black slim fit button down shirt with the top two buttons undone with the matching tuxedo jacket. He wore his hair completely slicked back without his signature part. His mask just covered the top of his face, made of black velvet fabric with red and gold brocade edging, and the top of each eye was pointed with shimmery red fabric. It reminded Jones of horns. It was quite devilish; however, it was also simple and sleek. Just the way Jones liked it.

Benny would meet them at the venue with the extra security, so Jones agreed to share transportation with Cam and Eden. Plus, the ladies would feel more comfortable on their first time at the ball. Farren was getting ready at their penthouse and he couldn't wait until he laid eyes on her. One thing Jones was certain of... they would *not* be sharing a ride home.

———

Jones parked his Mercedes G-wagon in the underground parking of Camedon's building. His footsteps echoed in the silence of the empty lot. He had a weird sensation that someone was watching him. His heartrate picked up, adrenalin kicking in preparing him for a fight. Jones slowed his footsteps to more closely take in his surroundings. Jones felt the urge to reach for his piece, but once again he had left it locked up in his vehicle.

I either need to stop being so damn paranoid, or carry my Glock on me all the fucking time.

Jones made his way to the elevator, and impatiently punched in the code for the penthouse. He didn't see or hear anyone following him, but he knew to trusts his instincts. He may not have seen anybody, but somebody was definitely there.

While in the elevator, Jones sent off a text to have reinforcements sent to the penthouse. He was more than capable of keeping Farren safe, and Cam always had his back, but he just wouldn't take the chance. Tobin Hunter was a dangerous fucker, and he had fallen off the radar as soon as Jones found out his identity.

Hunter must've had his own contacts working for him because as soon as Jax's friends had gotten back with a hit on the identity of Peter Ryan's killer, he all but disappeared. However, it wouldn't be so easy for him this time, because Benny had secured video footage of him talking to the mayor. There was now proof that they were connected, but the questions were how and why?

The elevator came to a smooth stop on the top floor of the swanky building, and Jones' heartrate picked up for a different reason. He was about to see Farren and he couldn't wait. He felt like a teenager on his first date. It was a weird effect that she had on him, but he was beginning to accept it.

"Honey, I'm home," Jones yelled as he made his way through the large living area. He immediately saw Cam standing at the floor to ceiling windows with a tumbler in his hand.

"Why are you yelling in my damn house you ginger bastard?" Cam turned to face Jones a scowl on his face, but mirth colored his blue-gray eyes.

"You want me to kick your ass? I told you about that ginger shit." Jones chuckled as he made his way to the bar.

"Yeah okay." Cam chuckled in return.

"You better be glad I'm looking so dapper. I don't want to get my suit all ruined before I take my baby out on the town," Jones stated as he dusted imaginary dust off his shoulder.

"Your baby, huh?" Cam smirked. "So this thing between you two is serious?"

"Hell yeah! I'm going to wife her ass, she just doesn't know it yet." Jones' tone conveyed the seriousness of his statement.

"Wow, never thought I'd see the day." Cam hesitated before he continued, "Well, as your best friend and the boyfriend to her best friend, you better not fuck this up. We've been friends for too long for me to have to cut your ginger ass off. And you know I will, after I beat your ass if you break Farren's heart."

Jones knew that Cam was only half joking. Hell, he understood. If the tables were turned, he would warn Cam against hurting Eden in a heartbeat. To find women like Farren and Eden was a miracle. They were intelligent, ambitious, successful, and beautiful. Farren had a heart of gold and was a fierce protector of everyone she loved. He'd be a damn fool for treating her any different than the queen that she was.

Jones was still surprised that she even gave him a chance in the first place. He was well aware that this was her first interracial relationship, and he was bound and determined it was going to be her one and only. Shit, he wanted to be her last relationship period.

He knew that it was early for him to even be thinking in long terms, but he didn't care. Jones knew that he wanted a forever kind of love with Farren even if they hadn't said the words to each other yet. They would get there, and he couldn't wait for the day.

"Earth to Jones." Cam waved his hands in front of Jones' face.

Jones shook his head to come back to the present. He was so lost in his thoughts that he didn't even hear Cam move.

"Everything alright with you buddy?" Cam asked with a curious expression.

"Lotta shit on my mind. I'm fine though, but I did want to update you on what was going on with Hunter," Jones finally replied with a heavy sigh.

"Ahh shit." Cam shook his head as he made his way to the bar to refresh his drink. "You better make this fast. The girls will be ready any minute."

Jones waved his hands dismissively. "They'll be another hour at least."

They both chuckled as they settled in. Jones proceeded to tell Cam all of the details about Tobin Hunter, and what they knew so far. The fact that he was a former hired killer was worrisome. However, even more troublesome was that he had left very little trace of his whereabouts in general.

Cam suggested that they call Jake Cameron, an old friend that was a former SEAL with a private investigation company, to help, but Jones knew that Jake had cut back on his work since his wife had their twins. He would only call him as a last resort. But for now, they would take care of everything themselves.

Approximately forty-five minutes later, the ladies emerged looking like goddesses. Eden was wearing a red dress that stood out against her ebony complexion. She wore a red and black silk mask that made her look both sweet and sinful at the same time, but once Farren entered the room, it was like time had stopped along with his heart.

Farren was wearing a sequined gold mini dress. It had spaghetti straps, and a deep V-neck design with an open back. The swirls of gold sequins lay over a sheer see through material that had peekaboo details on all of her naughty spots. She wore gold stilettoes with straps around the ankles that had to be at least six inches. Her brown hair was left down with big barrel curls that touched her shoulders, and the look was topped off with a delicate black lace mask decadent with embellishments of shimmery gold jewels. Her plump lips were decorated with a shimmery gold gloss, and Jones was instantly enthralled.

"Fuck, Sugar... you look good enough to eat."

Chapter Twenty-Four

TOBIN HUNTER/MURDERER

"Detective Carson is the problem in this investigation. He just won't let it go that Matthew Hughes was innocent of this murder. I tried to convince him to move on, but he just wouldn't." Detective Lawson tried to plead his case, but it was far too late for him. Tobin had already made up his mind that Lawson would be taken care of, and it was going to happen no matter how much he begged.

"He's *your* partner. I told you to take care of it. If somebody won't come to your side willingly, you convince them by other means. If you want to play with the big boys, you have to do what's necessary to win," Tobin replied as he looked the detective in his bruised and bloodied face.

Detective Lawson was sloppy and that made him a liability. Tobin found out that he was caught planting evidence, so it was only a matter of time before he told everything he knew to save his own ass.

It's time to get rid of the bumbling detective.

"Please, Mr. Hunter, give me another chance. I fucked up, but I can make it right. I can make the witnesses go away. Please just give me a ch..."

Pfft. The bullet was a mere whisper as it passed through the silencer and into Detective Lawson's head.

"Getting rid of the witness. That's a great idea detective." Hunter spoke out loud as he placed the gun in his pocket and made a phone call.

"Cleanup crew to Westchester Street."

―――――

FARREN

Farren was full of nervous energy and when she saw Jones, she was floored. His muscular frame was draped in a black traditional tuxedo that he somehow made look absolutely sinful. His auburn hair was neatly gelled away from his face, and his neatly trimmed beard surrounded his pink kissable lips. Her eyes roamed over his body until they locked onto his bright hazel eyes that were alight with mischief. Jones looked absolutely delicious, and the need to rip all of his clothes off and jump him right where he stood increased exponentially. Farren had a feeling that she would get to play out all of the erotic fantasies tonight, and she couldn't wait.

The chauffeured driven vehicle was filled with anticipation. Both couples laughed and teased one another, but Farren wasn't fooled by the easy banter. She knew that she wasn't the only person whose nerves were on edge. Jones played it cool on the outside, but she knew him too well. The way his hand aimlessly rubbed up and down her leg, and how his knee bounced up and down rapidly were his tells.

The conversation gave way to the anticipatory energy, and the silence shrouded the interior of the car. Farren nervously watched the scenery pass as they rode to the location, and she noticed that the warehouse was in a locale on the outskirts of Dallas. It was odd because it was if someone started a project and then left it incomplete. The building stood alone surrounded by a huge cement wall in the middle of nowhere.

The car pulled up to a private gate, and the driver punched in a code. The ride down the short driveway seemed like it took forever, but once the warehouse came into view, Farren was blown away.

The white building was lit by spotlights that turned blue, then golden brown, and then an orange reminiscent of flames of a fire. The colors represented the theme of the party; heaven, earth, and hell. There were three large guards standing in all black wearing simple black masks with ear pieces like they were the FBI.

"Wow, this is something." Farren looked at the building with awe in her voice.

"Just you wait, sweetheart. This is only the entrance." Camedon smiled as he took Eden's hand and led them inside with a nod to security.

When they entered the massive space, there was a petite brunette behind a massive counter that looked like a hotel check-in desk. She smiled brightly as they approached.

"Hi Jones, Cam. I'm so glad you guys are here finally. Everything is set and going well. There was a small ruckus earlier, but Benny took care of it. He can give you all the details when you have a moment."

"Great, thanks Savanah. I'll be sure to find Benny and see what's going on," Jones replied to his cheery assistant.

"I'm sure there's no need. It was just some ladies trying to get in that weren't on the list."

"Well I don't know how they found out about the party if they weren't on the list, but we'll get it taken care of. Thanks Savanah," Camedon spoke up.

They exchanged pleasantries with Jones' assistant for a few more minutes, but Farren couldn't even concentrate on what was being said, she was so giddy to get into the venue she was damn near dancing in place.

"You ready for this, Sugar?" Jones questioned his eyes peeking out beneath the velvet mask.

"As ready as I'll ever be." Farren took a deep breath but nothing could prepare her for what was behind the two massive doors.

Farren's jaw dropped open in astonishment. The room was bathed in a golden glow. The area looked like an exotic tropical lounge. There were plants and vines covering the walls, and trees that looked as if they were growing straight out of the floor. Several water features were gracing the walls, and fountains were strategically placed throughout the room.

There were at least twenty round bedlike structures that were suspended from the ceiling. They were piled with soft fluffy brown and gold pillows and draped with gold shimmery fabric.

It looked like a floating oasis of beds. Each bed was in the center of a sleek leather sectional couch. It was obvious that the beds were for the exhibitionist and the sofas were for the voyeurs.

The décor was fabulous, but what held Farren's attention were the couples that were occupying the beds. There were several people that were in various stages of undress. Some couples were in the midst of seductive foreplay, and others watched intently.

Farren surveyed the room with curious eyes. She didn't know where she wanted to look first. The waiters and waitresses were clad in almost nonexistent outfits, with elaborate bronze masks that covered the entire top part of their faces. Her eyes bounced from couples engaged in naughty displays of foreplay, to the sexy voyeurs whose lust filled eyes followed all of the action.

"Wow, just wow," Farren heard Eden whisper beside her.

Both men chuckled, but Farren knew that her and her bestie were on the same page.

"So I take it you like the décor?" Jones smirked his mask partially hiding his expression.

"Yeah, the décor is great, but... damn!" Farren replied with heat rising in her cheeks.

"This is just 'Earth', things aren't really kicked off in here. Now... we can go to heaven first or hell. What will it be ladies?" Cam questioned.

Farren thought that the ball would be a larger version of Euphoria, but the club had nothing on this place. At Euphoria, people were able to live out their fantasies. However, most took advantage of the private rooms, or like Farren, the rooms where you couldn't see the people that were watching you. But this room was all out in the open, everything put out there for everyone to see.

"Let's go up. We can always go *down* later." Farren smiled wickedly at Jones whose eyes gleamed with devilish intent.

Chapter Twenty-Five

JONES

As they rode the elevator up to the third floor, Jones started to feel himself relax. With all the security they had in place at the venue, there was no way that Tobin Hunter could get to Farren.

Jones decided that he would enjoy having his woman by his side for an important night for their company. Euphoria was a huge money maker, and the annual masquerade event helped to secure financial backing for many of their other ventures.

When the elevator stopped on the third floor, Jones looked directly at Farren to watch for her facial expressions. Her honey brown eyes went wide behind her mask, and they lit up with excitement. This floor was not like the lounge vibe of the "Earth" floor; this floor was about Heaven. This floor was about joy.

The décor was reminiscent of a space in Euphoria. Everything was white with a blue glow. There was a large white dance floor in the middle, it was surrounded by white couches and booths that lined the outside. The entire space was enclosed by white drapes that were also illuminated with a blue glow.

This space was about "the party." Everyone in Heaven was there to have a blast, and dance the night away. People were dressed in various styles, but they all wore masks as was the requirement. The staff in this section, wore white masks with white sheer outfits and of course, angel wings.

"Oh, so this is where the party is..." Farren smiled bobbing her head to the music.

"Come on Red, dance with me." Farren laughed as she pulled Jones' hand to lead him to the floor.

"I've told you about that 'Red' shit. Don't think you're not going to pay for that." Jones let her lead him to the floor. He wasn't a stellar dancer, and he sure as hell wasn't winning any contest, but he could do a little two step when necessary.

Jones and Farren danced a couple of songs until they stopped to get drinks. They settled into a booth to relax and drink when Camedon gave Jones a signal that they were going to slip out. Jones nodded and raised his glass.

There was no way the girls would get loose in front of one another, so it was inevitable that they eventually split up.

"Come on Sugar, let's go raise a little hell." Jones winked as he took Farren's hand.

———

When the doors opened on the bottom floor, the sight was the complete opposite of the top floor. Decadence and debauchery were the words that instantly came to mind.

Of course the room was decorated in shades of red and black, to match the devilish theme. There were black steel cages with partially naked men and women dancing behind the bars. Both, men and women, wore tiny leather bikini bottoms with chain link tops, and leather masks.

The entire floor of the space looked like one large bed, there were large pillows that looked like mattresses spread all over the room. They were all covered in red fabric that completed the look for the den of iniquity.

The music was melodic and soulful and filled the space with a lustful haze. People in this room came for one reason and one reason only... to fuck. The exhibitionists were out in full force, and everyone was putting on a show.

The elaborate masks were the only thing some people wore. The fervent displays of sex could make even the horniest of men blush. The outright demonstrations of sexual pleasure were overwhelming to every one of Jones' senses.

He had been holding back the feelings of want for Farren since he saw her come out in her shimmery gold dress. Jones had a lot of pent up energy, and he knew just how to expend it.

"It's time for you to pay the piper, Sugar," Jones whispered into Farren's ear. He watched as goosebumps covered her soft caramel skin.

"And just what type of payment are we talking about here?" Farren asked her voice low and husky.

"I want to see you strip for me."

Farren looked around the room with hesitation on her face. "Out here?"

"Oh no, baby. All those curves are only for me. You alright with that?" Jones' first concern was to make sure Farren was comfortable, and the hesitation he saw in her eyes showed that she wasn't completely comfortable with the idea of being out in the open.

Jones was okay with that; he didn't want to share her glorious body with anyone else. They would definitely have to have a conversation about the rules of their play time in public, but later. *Much later.*

Jones grabbed Farren's hand and led her through the room. She silently followed, and he saw that she was taking in all of the activities in the room. He watched as her face shadowed with lust and her eyes clouded with anticipation.

Once they reached their destination, Jones saw Farren visibly relax.

"Private room," Farren stated as she again took in her surroundings.

"Only the best for you. Now. Show your man what cha' got."

Jones took a seat in a large black leather chair that was pushed against a wall. The room had a circular bed that was draped with red fabric, and covered in plush black and red pillows. The opposite side of the room was covered in a floor to ceiling mirrors.

All of the private rooms were decorated in a similar fashion. Jones and Camedon spared no expense to get the warehouse looking like every fantasy they could think of. The warehouse wasn't just a venue for the masquerade, it was going to be their new location for Euphoria.

Farren walked slowly until she was standing right in front of him, just out of arms reach.

Smart move, Ms. Bell, Jones thought as he watched her intently.

She began to sway to the music that was pumping throughout the space. The song was slow and sultry. The tone was seductive, and he couldn't take his blazing eyes away from Farren's beautiful body.

She moved with a grace and elegance of royalty, each movement stirred Jones' want for her to a boiling level. Farren slowly started to slip the sequined dress from her body. She inched it over her succulent breasts, down her slightly rounded belly, until the material drifted with a sweet caress over her luscious hips. The dress glided to the floor, leaving her naked except for her gold mask and stilettoes.

Farren danced toward him slowly, she turned back to him and placed her hands on his knees, she shimmed her way down his seated body, and rubbed her round derriere across his rock hard cock in a way that made him want to lose control.

Farren continued to seduce him with her slow tantalizing gyrations. She stood up and bent down right in front of him. Her swollen lower lips dripping with her honey was right in front of his face. And he lost it.

Chapter Twenty-Six

FARREN

Farren was bent over, giving Jones an up close and personal view of her honey pot. When she felt his arm clamp around her in a vice grip, she knew that the beast had been released. Jones pulled her body backwards until his entire face was planted in her core from behind.

Jones breathed in deeply taking in her aroma, and Farren had to admit, it turned her on. He stuck out his tongue, and licked at her like a popsicle on a hot summer's day. Farren's body shook and convulsed uncontrollably when he pushed into her with a thick finger, and sucked on her clit. When the slurping sounds hit her ears, Farren screamed out in ecstasy.

"That's right baby. Lose it for your man. I love it when you give it to me." Jones' voice was gruff and full of a hunger that Farren had never heard before.

All Farren could do was moan, and let Jones control her body with his.

"Is it mine? Tell me I can have it." Jones turned her around and kissed her hard.

Words left her mind, all she could do was groan in pleasure at the sensations he was causing her body.

"I'm not going to be gentle with you, Farren." He continued, and she nodded her agreement still unable to form a cohesive sentence.

Jones carried her to the bed and sat her down on her feet. He slowly caressed her body until he was kneeling in front of her. He gently took each of her shoes off her feet, massaging them as he removed them. to massage and rub her, lulling her with his soft spoken words.

"I'm going to fuck you until your throat is raw, and then I'm going to fuck you some more."

Farren finally found her voice. "Well, that doesn't sound like punishment to me."

"Oh, honey. It's the best kind of punishment." Jones turned Farren around to face the bed. "Face down ass up. It's time to give me that sweet pussy."

Farren couldn't tell you how Jones got undressed so fast, but before she knew it, he was thrusting into her like a savage beast. This most definitely was not the soft love making that they've been doing lately, it wasn't even the passionate sex that they'd had in the past. This was raw, dirty, and unrestrained lust.

Farren could feel the power behind each and every one of his strokes. The long slow ones, the short quick ones, and definitely the ones she could feel in her chest. She lost count of how many times she climaxed, and when Jones finally yelled out her name in ecstasy, she could've sworn they'd been at it for hours.

As they lay in the bed, in post coital bliss, Farren felt more relaxed than she had in months. She needed to lose herself, and let go of her inhibitions, and Jones helped her to do that.

Jones did everything that he promised, he protected her, cared for her, and supported her without asking for anything in return. He was one of the only men that ever kept his word to her and it meant the world.

I'm in love with Jones Sullivan.

———

After they cleaned themselves up, Jones gave Farren a short tour of the rest of the facility that was finished. She was surprised to find out that they were relocating Euphoria, but the space was perfect. She was having fun and was able to relax more, but there were the unspoken feelings that Farren could sense between them.

She wouldn't be the cliché girl about her feelings, and pretend she didn't have them. Farren was an outspoken woman, and love it or hate it, she wore her heart on her sleeve. She would talk to Jones about how she felt, and they could face it together head on, whether he felt the same way about her or not; just like they did with the talk of birth control.

The first time they had had unprotected sex, it caught her off guard. Jones showed her his most recent tests, and Farren did the same. They talked about what they both wanted, and felt comfortable with. She had to admit that she wasn't excited about the prospect of going back to condoms after she had felt Jones skin to skin.

They both came to the conclusion that she would get the birth control implant, and when it took effect, they wouldn't use condoms. Farren was going to get an implant anyway since she couldn't remember to take her pill, so it was the logical conclusion.

Now all she had to find out was what had been bothering Jones for the past couple of weeks, and they would be back on track. But she would save that for another time. Tonight, had gone to well for her to bring up the tension that she had noticed in him.

They didn't see Cam or Eden for the rest of the night which Farren was sort of happy about. She loved her best friend, and they shared a lot of things together; but seeing Eden in all of her glory having sex was not something Farren wanted to sign up for.

They were getting ready to go for the night after Jones checked with his assistant, and made sure that the security was still in place. Farren now understood a lot better all of the things that went into running a successful club. It was time to go because the party was winding down, and since Jones had been drinking, and they were both tired Benny drove them home.

Farren was snuggled in Jones' arms dozing off. There was no other place that she'd rather be than in his arms. He always held her as if she were the most precious of jewels. He treated her like a queen, and she felt safe and comforted in his arms.

Farren was sleeping sound when the screeching of tires woke her with a fright. She sat up and looked around frantically, but before she could ask what was going on Jones was in protector mode.

"Sit back and buckle your seatbelt, Farren. Hurry!" His voice held a sense of urgency, and his face was an angry mask.

Farren buckled her seat belt. "What the hell is going on?" She looked around desperate as she tried to figure out what was happening.

Benny jerked the wheel to the right then back to the left sharply. It felt as if the SUV would turn over. Farren yelled and held on for dear life. Just when she thought it couldn't get any worse, there was another SUV with dark tinted windows right next to them trying to run them off the road.

The SUV swerved swiping the side of their vehicle. Farren screamed. Jones yelled at Benny, but the blood rushing in her ears prevented her from hearing what was being said. Just when she didn't think things could get worse, gunshots rang out.

"Oh my God! They're shooting! Ohmigod Ohmigod!" Farren hysterically chanted over and over. She wanted to get in the floor, but what if they wrecked?

Farren could feel the tears streaming down her face unchecked, and her heart raced. She still didn't have a clue as to what was going on, or why.

Jones rolled down the window, and started to shoot at the other vehicle. Farren couldn't say she was surprised because she knew who he was, but she still couldn't believe she was in a certified shoot out.

How is this my fuckin' life right now? She thought as she ducked in her seat. She made herself as small as possible while being hindered by the seatbelt. She heard screeching tires once again followed by a loud crash.

Benny hit the brakes hard and the SUV tilted slightly before coming to an abrupt stop. Farren tried hard to get her sobbing under control, but she couldn't.

"Stay here, and stay down!" Jones shouted as he and Benny exited the car.

"No! Don't leave me here," Farren continued to sob as she reached for Jones. Benny continued toward the over turned vehicle.

"Farren, baby it will be fine. Just please stay here where you're safe. I'll be back." He gave her a kiss that was meant to reassure her but Farren couldn't calm down.

Before he could fully get out of the car, Farren heard shouting and another gunshot.

"Oh my God, Jones!" Farren shouted.

"Fuck, Benny!" Jones yelled as he took off running.

Chapter Twenty-Seven

JONES

The shots rang out loud in the eerie silence of the night. He saw Benny drop to the ground, and his blood went cold. Before he could even process what had happened, Jones' feet moved with precision. He was on autopilot, with his gun drawn he shot at the overturned SUV as he ran toward Benny.

Benny was on the ground, but he was alive. He returned gun fire until the night was silent again. Jones made it to Benny, and saw that he was hit in the stomach.

"Fuck, Ben. Shit! Hold tight for me. I need to get you some help." Jones took off his jacket covering Benny's wound.

Benny coughed but stayed silent. Jones didn't want to move him because he didn't know how bad the gunshot was. But he did a quick check to make sure he wasn't hit anywhere else.

"You hit anywhere else?" Jones questioned.

"Naw man, I don't think so." Benny coughed loudly. "Is Farren okay?" Benny coughed again, and this time blood came out of his mouth.

Jones knew that Benny was a good guy, and he wasn't surprised that he was worried about Farren's safety even though he was the one lying on the ground shot.

Jones heard hurried footsteps, and he knew instantly that Farren didn't do what he instructed. She'd gotten out of the car. *Hardheaded woman!*

"Oh shit, B-nice. Oh God! What can I do to help?" Farren fired off question after question, but at least she was no longer crying.

"Take my phone..."

"Okay, I'll call 911..."

"No!" Both Benny and Jones shouted in unison.

"Call my brother. He'll handle it.

"Okay, okay. Uh... which brother?" Farren questioned with wide eyes.

"Jax."

Jones noticed Farren's shaking hands as she dialed Jax's number, he knew that she was terrified, but he had to focus his attention on keeping Benny alive.

"Jax, it's Farren. There's been a situation, and we need you to get here as quickly as possible."

Jones was glad she didn't give details of what was going on over the phone. *My woman is a smart cookie.*

"Benny's been hurt bad. We need help now," Farren said after a few seconds.

"You can do that? Wow... okay, please hurry." Jones could only hear one side of the conversation, but it sounded like help was on the way. Farren disconnected the call, and turned her fear shaded eyes to him.

"Jax is on the way. He said he tracked your phone and he's ten minutes out."

"We can't wait for him. We need to get Benny some help." Jones started to get up. "We need to help Benny to the car, Jax can clean up this mess, but we have to go."

Jones stood, helping Benny to his feet. Farren ran to the other side of him and draped his long arm over her shoulder. It took a lot of strength and persistence, but they finally got Benny to their SUV.

Jones hit the number of an underground doctor that he knew as soon as he got into the vehicle. The Bluetooth connected on the second ring, and the doctor directed them to the nearest location.

There was no way Jones was going to a regular hospital with a gunshot victim. There would be too many questions, and there was at least one dead body at the scene. The police would be called, and there was no way in hell he could trust any of them.

Jax would clear the scene, and find out for certain who put the hit out on them. In the meantime, Benny would get the help he needed without having to involve law enforcement.

———

Jones had taken Benny to an exclusive underground care facility. The surgeon had immediately operated on Benny removing one bullet. Luckily, it missed all of the vital organs and Benny would make a full recovery.

Jones waited until after Benny was out of surgery and resting in a private room before he left for home. He didn't want to leave Benny alone, but he needed his rest, and there was nothing more Jones could do for him.

Jones made his way home with Farren in tow. It was a close call tonight, and he wasn't willing to let her out of his sight. Jax was waiting at his condo when they arrived, and he knew the night was not over.

Jax embraced Farren as soon as she made her way through the door. He pulled back with a look of brotherly affection covering his face.

"You okay?" Jax questioned.

"I will be as soon as you tell us what the hell is happening." Jones knew that Farren was a strong woman, but he would never again underestimate just how strong.

Once she saw that Benny was hurt, all tears were gone, and a look of determination covered her face. Although her hands still shook, and tears welled in her beautiful eyes, she never once faltered. And Jones was proud.

"Why don't you guys go get cleaned up, and I'll tell you everything I know," Jax answered.

Jones nodded and led Farren to his master bathroom. The night had started with so much potential, but it had gone down the drain quick. All he wanted to do was lose himself in Farren, hold her close and never let her go.

Jones and Farren undressed each other slowly and with reverence. They showered in silence as they bathed each other. Once they were finished and toweled dry, they dressed in comfort. Jones knew that whatever Jax had to say was going to be life changing, and he had to get ready to do whatever needed to be done.

"Thank you for saving my life, Jones. I just don't know where I'd be if it weren't for you." Farren broke the silence with her heartfelt words.

"I would do it a million times over, Farren." Jones pulled her into his arms in a warm familiar embrace. "Now let's go handle business."

"So I'm glad you guys are okay. But we have a lot of shit to discuss." Jax was all business and Jones was glad that he could once again count on his brother.

"Tobin Hunter was behind the hit tonight. And he isn't just some rogue ex-mercenary. He's a friend of the mayor, and is head of his personal security."

"How did we not know that he was the head of security for the fucking mayor? That should be easy information to find." Jones scooted forward in his seat as he tried to control his anger.

"Personal security is not something that has to be divulged. Even as mayor."

"That's complete bullshit! This man is a fucking hired killer! How the hell is it acceptable for him to be the mayor's security?" There was no mistaking the anger in Jones' voice.

"It's not well-known information what kind of man Tobin Hunter is. You know what it took to find that out..." Jax raised a brow at Jones, and Jones settled down some.

It took a lot of favors for Jax to find out who Tobin Hunter was, and Jones would forever be in debt of his brother.

"Listen, the man didn't live this long under the radar because he's stupid. He hides behind corporations and dummy businesses. We couldn't even find an account in his name."

"So what you're telling me is, a hired hitman is the mayor's personal bodyguard and he is out to kill *me* because I witnessed him kill the mayor's nephew?" Farren finally spoke up.

"That's it in a nutshell," Jax said dryly.

"Fuck my life." Farren sat back with a heavy sigh. "So you're going to have to kill him?"

"That would be a fair assessment of the situation. If he was even arrested and brought up on charges, he could disappear without a trace. You won't be safe until he's dead," Jax answered in an even tone.

"But if he's in bed with the mayor he would never be arrested," Farren stated, and Jones could hear the frustration in her voice.

"No, it wouldn't. We still aren't sure of the leaks in the police department, now with the mayor's direct involvement; this shit just got deep." Jax ran a hand through his brown hair, and Jones knew the frustration that his brother felt.

"So what do we do? And what about the gunmen from tonight?" Jones could hear the worry in Farren's voice with each question she asked, so he pulled her into his lap, and rubbed her back in a soothing motion. He needed to give her some comfort.

"Well, when Jones called me earlier tonight for more security, I took it upon myself to do a little tracking."

Jax went on to tell them how he had found a second car that had been tailing Jones at Cam's penthouse. With a little persuasion, along with a couple of punches, the man had been forthcoming about who he worked for, and the details of his mission.

The guy was just some lowlife weasel trying to make a quick buck. His job was to call Hunter whenever Jones and Farren left. There were other men that would follow them until they had the opportunity to carry out the hit. There was no way they could get into the venue, so they waited until Jones and Farren left to strike.

Jax was already on his way to the party when Farren called. When Jax got to the scene, there was one man dead and another on his way to meet the grim reaper. Jax was able to get identification from both men. It was obvious they weren't professionals, and Jax wondered why a man like Hunter would use such incompetent people.

Then it hit him, if they were successful then his witness problem was over. If they botched the job, then Farren would call the police and she would most likely be put under some kind of surveillance by the police, and Hunter would know exactly when to get to her. It was a win-win for Hunter, but he didn't count on Jones.

Jones was too smart to call the police, and now they had one up on Hunter. It was time to bring his ass down.

Chapter Twenty-Eight

FARREN

Farren was exhausted from the night's events. She was so excited about the masquerade ball and it was everything she thought it would be and more, but then everything had turned to shit.

Benny was recovering from a gunshot wound because of her. Some maniac tried to kill her because she was in the wrong place at the wrong time. Tobin Hunter was running around killing people left and right, and instead of him being behind bars, he was out there terrorizing her.

She couldn't even call the police for help. How in the hell was she supposed to live her life? How was she supposed to carry on with a lunatic out there? The questions plagued her, but at least she'd figured out what had been going on with Jones for the last few weeks.

"So you've been so distant because of this Hunter guy?" Farren asked Jones as they got ready for bed.

Jones sighed loudly, and she knew that it was more to it than what she thought.

"This guy isn't your run of the mill crazy person. He has skills that not many people possess. He is more dangerous than almost anyone I know."

"Almost?" Farren questioned curiously.

Jones smirked. "Jax," he stated simply, and Farren had a feeling that was a long conversation.

"So you kept all of this from me? You worried and stressed yourself out over me?" Farren's tone was accusatory. She couldn't believe that he would keep such vital information from her, but more importantly he carried the burden alone.

"I didn't have all the intel I needed on the guy. There was no need for both of us to be worried." Farren knew that Jones was the protector type, but she had no idea the lengths that he would go through until now.

"That's not who we are. You and I... we talk. You should've told me."

"I'm sorry, but telling you would've only made you upset, and I refuse to be the one to do that." Jones' voice was laced with conviction.

"I understand why you didn't tell me, but you should have." Farren sighed. "I thought you were having second thoughts about us." Farren's words were soft. She hated that her insecurities showed.

"Oh, Sugar. I would never have second thoughts about us. I love you too damn much to be that damn stupid." Jones' face was filled with sincerity, and Farren's heart skipped a beat.

"I love you too, Red." Farren smiled as she flung herself into his arms and kissed him passionately.

After their kiss died down to pecks of affection, Farren couldn't help but feel a little relieved. Although the situation was less than ideal, she and Jones had found each other, and she was thankful for that.

"Let's get some rest. We'll need to go see Benny tomorrow, and Jax and I have some things we need to do."

"Okay, but you guys need to be careful," Farren stated simply.

"Don't worry, Sugar. I'll be safe, so I can keep you safe. Now let's get some sleep."

Farren snuggled into Jones' body, and again she thought that there was no place she'd rather be. Now they just had to get rid of the psycho killer and maybe she could get her life back to normal.

———

TOBIN HUNTER

"Look, Philip, you are the reason I'm in such a mess. That idiot nephew of yours wouldn't have been able to blackmail you if you could keep your dick in your pants." Hunter pointed at Mayor Ryan.

"Just because we're old friends, doesn't mean you can talk to me that way," the mayor responded. "I hired you to do a job because I know that you're the best, but you've fucked this thing up from the beginning."

"I had to kill your nephew that night. He was on his way to meet with a journalist with evidence of your affair with a girl that was barely eighteen. He had video proof. There's no coming back from that. I've invested too much time and money into you for you to go down and take me with you."

"I didn't say killing Peter was a mistake. Being seen was the mistake you made. You've never been seen before. You killed Peter in a public place. That was stupid, and you know it."

"Peter was always surrounded by people. I told you I had to take the opportunity when it was presented to me."

Tobin was tired of explaining himself. If he wasn't so invested in his old friend's political future, he would've killed him and his nephew and cut all ties with the Ryan family. However, if Philip Ryan was able to have a successful run as mayor, then the governor's office would be next. The political connections for a hired hitman was a goldmine. So he had to cleanup all of Philip's messes, including his addict nephew that wanted money for his gambling and drugs.

"The guy the cops tried to pin the murder on had the charges against him dropped, so what now?"

"I'll have the witnesses taken care of just like I have with everyone else."

"What about Detective Lawson? Is he going to be a problem, and his partner?" Philip questioned.

"Detective Lawson has been dealt with. Everyone will think he's on the run because he was caught planting evidence. They will look for him, but they'll never find him. His case just like your nephew's will go cold."

———

There was one witness left, and Tobin was having one hell of a time getting to her. Farren Bell had become a major kink in his plan. The other two witnesses were easy. They were drunk concert goers, but they saw him coming out of the alley. However, they had already taken money to finger another person. There was no way they would come forward to incriminate themselves any further, and if they did, he would kill them.

Philip was right, killing Peter in that alley was a major fuck up on his part. He was a highly trained killer, and never, not once had he made such bad decisions. He had been following Peter for days, and never had the chance to get him alone.

It was of great importance that nobody else knew what was going on, so he couldn't trust anybody to do the job.

The stress of the situation had gotten the best of him, and before he knew it he'd had one too many drinks, and then he'd run across Peter making a drug deal. When the other man left, he had taken advantage of Peter being in a dark alley by himself.

He had been careless, and he was paying for it big time. Tobin knew never to drink on the job, and in his twenty plus years he'd never made that mistake. But all he had to do to correct everything was to kill one woman, and soon, it would be over.

Tobin knew what he had to do. He had to get Farren Bell when she least expected it. He had to go to a place where she felt safe, and when her guard was down, he knew just what he had to do.

Chapter Twenty-Nine

JONES

Jones hated to leave Farren alone, but after they visited Benny he could tell she was still exhausted. He was well aware of the guilt she was feeling, and he didn't want her carrying that around. Jones had been through feeling guilty, and that was the last thing he wanted for Farren. He wanted to give her some time and space, so he took her back to his house to let her rest while he and Jax met with their old friend, Officer Linda Michaels.

Linda had been quiet, and for good reason. Apparently, internal affairs were cracking down on all of the leaks in the department. They had even found out that Detective Lawson had tampered with evidence, and now all of his cases were under review. He and his partner, Detective Carson were under investigation. Jones was surprised at the revelation because according to Farren it was Detective Carson that seemed like the dirty cop. So to hear that Lawson was the dirty one, shocked Jones.

Apparently, things got worse for the detective after two witnesses were brought in, and they both pointed the finger at the same innocent person for Peter Ryan's murder. Someone took notice. Matthew Hughes wasn't exactly a squeaky clean suspect. He had numerous arrests for drugs and theft, but he had never been a violent criminal.

However, he did fit the description; he was tall with blonde hair and ice blue eyes. The only problem with him was that at the time of the murder, he was on camera at a convenient store robbing the clerk at gunpoint.

It was a bogus arrest, and they had to drop the murder charges. The information wasn't released because Matthew was booked on robbery charges, and was still in jail.

Now that Jones knew that the detectives were dirty, there was no wonder why they didn't call Farren in for the line-up. They'd planned to put Matthew Hughes away for the murder, and close their case with a neat little bow. If Lawson wouldn't have been caught on camera planting evidence, nobody would've even questioned the veteran officer.

According to Linda, Farren's name wasn't even included in the main case file of the Ryan case. So that meant that Lawson was definitely the person responsible for giving Tobin Hunter all of Farren's information.

Jones wanted to beat the shit out of Lawson. The only problem was; nobody had seen him in over a week. Linda, as well as the rest of the department, assumed he was on the run. However, Jones knew better; Lawson was dead. If he was working with Hunter, and he was missing now that things were getting hot, there wasn't a chance in hell that he was still alive.

The meeting with Linda was very informative. It answered a lot of questions that Jones had about why the case was moving so slow. However, there were questions that still remained; like why did the mayor want his nephew dead? And where the hell was Tobin Hunter?

Jones didn't have a clue as to where to start to find Hunter. But he knew exactly where to find the mayor.

————

The mayor was all too happy to take a last minute meeting with the Sullivan brothers. After all, they were multimillionaires and from old money. They were just the type of people that could contribute big bucks to his upcoming campaign.

If he would've listen to Hunter, he would've known that Jones Sullivan was not somebody he would ever want to be in a meeting with, and Jax Sullivan was definitely someone he didn't want to be in the same room with.

"Gentlemen, come on in and have a seat," Mayor Ryan offered with a flourish.

Both Jax and Jones smirked at one another before taking the offered chairs. The mayor's office in his home was very telling of what type of man he was. It was gaudy and overstated, like he was trying entirely too hard to show his wealth.

"What can I do for you today?" Mayor sat down behind his massive desk.

"Where's Tobin Hunter?" Jax cut straight to the chase, and by the look on the mayor's face, he wasn't expecting the question.

"I don't know who that is." The mayor lied smoothly, but not smooth enough.

Jones pulled the still pictures from the video Benny took, and slid them across the desk. The mayor's face lost all color as he went pale.

"Where did you get these?" Mayor Ryan questioned.

"I'm going to ask you one more time, where is Tobin Hunter?" Jax slid forward in his chair and placed his hands on the desk.

"I don't know where he is. I never know where he is."

"Why did he kill your nephew?" Jones questioned.

"Again, I don't know what you're talk..."

The mayor was unable to finish his sentence because Jones pulled out a gun with a silencer, and placed it on the desk. He was not about to play this game with the mayor. He didn't have the time or the patience. He would kill him without a second thought.

"I *will* kill you."

"Yo- you wou- wouldn't," the mayor stammered, his eyes going wide.

"I most certainly would." Jones picked up the gun and pointed at the mayor's head.

"And I would make it look like a suicide. So tell us where Hunter is, and don't fuck around or you'll be dead before you can finish the lie," Jax commented.

The mayor told a tale of blackmail, drug addiction, and murder. Peter Ryan and a girl he gave drugs to had a scheme to get money from his uncle. The girl was barely eighteen and Peter had convinced her that their little plan would work. And it did.

It was easy to seduce the mayor and have an affair because the man was a narcissistic asshole that couldn't keep his dick in his pants. His nephew set up a hidden camera in the mayor's home office, and the rest is history.

Peter had extorted over twenty thousand dollars from him until he upped the ante and demanded one hundred thousand. That was when the mayor let his head of security know what was going on. Hunter was already invested in the mayor's future, and he was an old friend, so he knew that Hunter would help him.

First, the girl was found dead of an apparent overdose, and nobody ever questioned it. So Ryan entrusted Hunter to take care of his nephew as well. And that was where the mistakes started to happen.

The story was so outlandish that Jones could hardly believe his ears, but the weasel was too afraid to lie to them while he was staring down the barrel of a gun, so Jones was inclined to believe him.

"That's some tale, mayor. I hope the police actually believe you when you turn yourself in," Jax stated after the mayor was finished talking.

"No- now wait just one minute. That wasn't part of the deal." The mayor looked between the two with wide disbelieving eyes.

"I don't remember making a deal. Do you?" Jones looked at Jax for an answer.

"Nope. Can't say that I remember that either," Jax replied with a smile.

"I'm not ruining my career behind this. Nobody will ever believe you two. Like you said it's an unbelievable story." Mayor Ryan sat back in his chair with a look of triumph coloring his pudgy red face.

Jones removed a small recorder from his pocket, and began the playback of the mayor's voice. The man's face turned pale once more at the realization that he was not going to get away with murder.

"You have two choices. You can turn yourself in, or I can send this tape to the local news station. As a matter of fact, I know a DJ that would love to broadcast this on her show." Jones' face broke out in a satisfied smile as the mayor gulped loudly.

The mayor lowered his head in resignation. "Fine I'll turn myself in, but under my terms."

The brothers laughed. "You don't run shit, Mr. Mayor. You're turning yourself in now."

"You can laugh all you want to, but you won't be laughing when Hunter gets through with you," the mayor spat out snidely.

There was something in his voice that made Jones pause for a brief moment. He had an idea of where Hunter was, and he needed to get there fast.

"Jax, you take care of this. I need to get to Farren." Jones didn't wait for a response as he ran full speed out of the mayor's office.

Chapter Thirty

TOBIN HUNTER

It wasn't that hard to bypass security in the upscale high-rise building, especially since he'd spent the last few days casing the place. The snooty manager was very efficient at his job, and he wanted everyone who entered the building to know that he was in charge, so it was easy to catch him in the underground parking garage. The man didn't resist at all. He gave Hunter everything he needed to get into Jones Sullivan's condo.

Too bad his cooperation wasn't able to save his life. Hunter had learned a valuable lesson from this situation; never ever leave loose ends.

Hunter donned a pair of coveralls, a blue baseball cap, and carried a tool box all under the guise of being a repair man. He strolled through the lobby as if he belonged. He made his way to the elevator when he heard someone shout at him.

"Fuck," Hunter mumbled under his breath.

"Hey! Sir! You're using the wrong elevator," a young man called out coming from behind a large desk in the lobby.

"I'm sorry. What?" Hunter questioned as he pulled the bill of his cap down and covered his face more.

"You must be new... that's okay. Our manager likes for repair men to use the staff elevator in the back. It creates an illusion that nothing ever needs to be fixed." The young man rolled his eyes in obvious contempt of his manager.

"Oh right. Like you said, I'm new and wasn't sure where that elevator was," Hunter replied as he tried to sound casual, but this conversation was already dragging out for too long. He didn't need to be seen on any cameras.

"Not a problem." The young man pointed at a hallway by the doors. "You can use those since you're already in the lobby, but on the way out make sure you use the elevators by the exit doors. Those are for staff."

"Will do. Thanks buddy." Hunter walked quickly in the direction of the staff elevators. The encounter actually served a purpose. Now he had an easier way out of the building, and would be less likely to be seen.

The elevator didn't stop, so the ride up to the top floor of the building was a smooth one. Hunter made his way down the hall in search of the right door. Once he found it, he pulled out the stolen master key, and unlocked the door.

His entrance into the spacious condo was silent. Hunter shut the door with a whisper. He placed the toolbox down and pulled out the gun he had hidden inside. He took out the silencer and screwed it onto the gun.

The apartment was quiet, and there wasn't any sign of anyone being there. The TV was off, and there was no movement anywhere. Hunter moved to the kitchen, and there was no one there either. He made his way back to the living room when suddenly the lights flashed on then off. Hunter paused his movements, he went on alert instantly. He looked around, and didn't see anything out of the ordinary. After a few minutes, nothing happened so he proceeded this time with even more caution. The last thing he needed was to alert anyone of his presence.

Hunter made his way down a long hall where he checked a guest bedroom and bathroom. He checked two more bedrooms and found nothing. Farren Bell wasn't there. Hunter knew that she had to be in the building somewhere. He saw her, and Sullivan enter the building, and later when he left, she was not with him.

"Fuck!! Where the fuck is she!" Hunter raged.

I'll tear this place apart until I find where she went. Hunter thought as he made his way through the large luxury apartment in a blind fury.

———

FARREN

Farren had been resting in bed when the lights flashed on and off. She automatically began to move because she knew what was happening, and she was absolutely terrified. She never thought that she would be there to witness the silent alarm going off in Jones' apartment. Farren quickly moved to the back of the closet in the master bedroom, and entered the number on the hidden keypad. The door quietly opened to the secret security room, and Farren made her way inside.

When Jones had shown her the room, she had laughed at him and told him he was the most paranoid person she knew. Farren never knew anyone to take security as seriously as Jones did, but now with Tobin Hunter in the apartment obviously there to kill her, she would eat all the crow in the world.

Jones made sure that she knew all the codes to everything, and he walked her through the process almost every time she entered the apartment. He made sure that she knew what to do in the small chance there was ever an intruder. Farren didn't understand why he had so many extra security measures because the building itself was so secure. But now she understood.

With a brother like Jax, Jones would know that there were people with skills to get past the building security. And with everything that happened to Cam and Eden, Farren could see and she understood Jones' overprotective need for the security.

Farren watched on the security cameras as Hunter raged and stomped his way through each room. It was lucky that she'd grabbed her phone on her way into the closet. She sent out a text to Jones to let him know what was happening.

Farren: he's here!

Jones: I know baby... OTW

Farren: YOU KNOW!!! WTF???

Jones: Sit tight. Don't move...

Jones: I mean it Farren! Don't move!!!!

"Damn, did he have to use so many exclamation points? I'm not that dang hardheaded," Farren mumbled petulantly.

Farren wasn't certain of how much time had passed, but when she saw Jones enter through the front door, her heart stopped. He was alone, and his gun led the way through the opened front door.

She wanted to yell at him to call the police, or even Jax. The last thing Farren wanted was for Jones to be by himself to save her. If he got hurt, or worse, she would never be able to forgive herself.

It was as if time had slowed down when Jones entered the room Hunter was in. The men faced each other down with their weapons drawn. It was as if Farren was watching some modern day western. Her hands shook, and her brow was covered in sweat. The fear was almost nauseating.

"Shit, what are they saying?" Farren couldn't hear anything but she could see their lips move, and before she knew it, there was a popping sound.

"Jones!!!" She screamed as she headed to the door of the room.

Chapter Thirty-One

JONES

Jones couldn't believe the audacity of the motherfucker standing in front of him. Tobin Hunter needed to die. He had wrecked enough havoc on Farren's life to last an eternity, and it was going to end today one way or another.

"So Jones Sullivan to the rescue. Is that it?" Hunter questioned, his gun pointed at Jones' head.

Jones tilted his head to the side and looked the man up and down. There weren't many things in this world that could cause Jones to go into a blind fury, but this man was able to accomplish that with very little effort.

"One of us is going to die here to..." The bullet that went between Hunter's eyes stopped him midsentence, and his body fell to the floor with a loud thud.

Jones had no time to talk with this motherfucker. He was not about to sit and have conversation and tea.

"Who the fuck did you think I was?" Jones said to the dead man as he took his gun.

One thing Jones didn't play about was his family, and Farren was definitely family. He heard her screaming his name as she ran in the direction of his office.

"I told you not to move!" Jones caught a sobbing Farren as she launched her body at his.

"Why the hell are you by yourself?" Farren slapped his chest then kissed his lips before she slapped his chest again.

"What? I can't protect my woman on my own?" he asked with a cocked brow.

"Not the point, Red." She kissed him again.

"What'd I tell you about that 'Red' shit?" Jones questioned as he pulled Farren into his arms and away from his office.

There was no need for her to be traumatized anymore by the bastard. He closed the door and led Farren to the family room. There were going to be a lot of questions, and this time, he had to call the police.

To be a highly trained killer, he sure was a fuck up, Jones thought as he took the phone out of his pocket and dialed the police.

Jax was the first person to show up, and he wasn't happy that Jones had to kill Hunter. No matter how old they got, Jax would always treat him like his *little* brother. He didn't want any of his brothers to be killers, even though almost all of them already were.

Jax pulled Jones into a brotherly embrace. "You alright?"

"I'm good. Just glad this shit is finally over."

Jones was serious about this being over. He didn't want Farren to have to live another day fighting this battle. He knew that Hunter had to die in order for that to happen, so he'd pulled the trigger without a second thought.

After the police asked some questions and viewed the surveillance video, it was a pretty clear cut case of self-defense. Of course, there would be a process before that was an official ruling, but Jones wasn't worried about that.

Jones saw that Farren was finished answering questions, and she was no longer crying. Although she was visibly shaken, the relief that covered her gorgeous face was a beautiful sight to see.

He made his way over to her and pulled her into his lap. Jones nuzzled her neck, and she sighed audibly. The contentment he felt having her safe and sound wrapped in his arms overwhelmed him.

"How you doin', Sugar?"

"Better now. I can't believe after six months, it's over."

"Believe it."

"Can we... uh, stay somewhere else tonight? I know it's safe, but you shot him..." Farren's voice was hesitant, but Jones understood completely.

"We can go wherever you want, Sugar." Jones kissed her lips softly, and he knew that he would take her anywhere in the world.

FARREN

Farren couldn't describe the freedom and happiness she felt now that Tobin Hunter was gone. His pale blue eyes had haunted her dreams for months, and she was glad that a dangerous man was off the streets.

The mayor was involved in a huge scandal, and resigned his position after turning himself in for conspiracy to commit murder. Of course Jax was there to make sure that he "did the right thing."

Farren couldn't believe that she had wasted all of that time feeling sorry for the mayor, and he was the one behind his own nephew's death. He was a despicable and disgusting man, and jail was too good for the likes of him.

It had only been a few days since everything had happened. She had taken off work to clear her head after everything she'd been through. She hadn't had any more problems out of Evan, but she felt like it was time to move on.

Benny was still recuperating although he was doing much better, and Farren had to admit that she missed her friend's smiling face and the banter between them. She was just happy that he was going to make a full recovery.

With everything that had happened, Farren still hadn't been back to Jones'. In fact, she hadn't returned home either. But he wouldn't let her out of his sight, so for the last couple of nights they stayed at the W hotel in downtown Dallas.

"Are you ready yet? We're gonna be late," Jones yelled through the suite.

"We're not going to be late. And YES, I'm ready." Farren came out of the bedroom wearing a simple white t-shirt with blue wide-legged pants.

They were meeting their friends for dinner to catch up. Now that a killer was off the streets, and Farren felt like she wouldn't be putting the people she loved in unnecessary danger, she could relax and enjoy her loved ones.

Twenty minutes later, they walked arm and arm into Kenichi, an Asian restaurant within walking distance from the W. When they arrived, their group of friends were all there, being rowdy, and laughing loudly.

"Well if it isn't the happy couple?" Harper spoke first as he rose from his chair to give Farren a hug.

When Harper hugged her a little too long, Jones stepped up and pulled him away. Of course, Harper, being the trouble maker that he was, blew kisses at Farren as he pretended to struggle to get back to her.

"Oh my goodness, Harp, you are so dramatic." Farren laughed as she greeted the rest of the group.

"Where's Elyse?" She questioned once they were settled in with their drinks.

"She said she was on her way. You know how Elyse is," Eden answered.

Everyone was comfortable and enjoying the camaraderie when Elyse made her grand entrance. Farren almost spit out her drink, and on instinct, her eyes went to Harper. His face flashed with a deep scowl before it was replaced with a blank expression.

Farren had no idea what was going on between the two of them, but Elyse walking in with a date said a lot.

Farren and Eden looked at each other with a "girl, no she didn't" look.

"Hey Lysee, I'm glad you could make it," Farren stated as she hugged Elyse.

"You know I wouldn't miss this." Elyse winked. "Farren, you remember Travis. We met him at the charity event a couple of weeks ago."

Farren nodded in recognition. The sexy guy with the bright green eyes.

"Nice to see you again." Travis shook her hand.

Elyse introduced her date to everyone, and the conversation resumed. The tension between Elyse and Harper was palpable. But Farren pretended she was Kermit...

That's none of my business.

The night was just what Farren needed, the love that she felt from her friends was wonderful, and she would be forever grateful for their support.

EPILOGUE

JONES

"Sugar, are you ready yet?" Jones was forever waiting on Farren to get ready, but he would wait until the ends of time for her. He just liked to give her a hard time about her beauty routine.

"Red, can you chill the hell out? I'll be ready in a second. I'm already nervous and you're making it worse!" Farren yelled from the bathroom.

They weren't officially living together yet. They had only been seeing each other for eight months, but Jones wanted to get a new place after everything that had happened. He knew Farren wasn't comfortable staying in a place where he killed a man, and Jones completely understood that. So he put his place on the market, which sold within a week, and he was staying with her until he found a place.

Really he was trying to convince her to move in with him, and he hadn't quite gotten her to agree yet. But he would.

"Sugar, I'm sure you look great. My family is going to love you. I promise."

"You have to say that because you love me." Farren pouted as she finally came out of the bathroom and she looked good enough to eat.

"You know I have *six* brothers. Do you expect me to fight them all?" He questioned with a serious expression.

Farren had on a tight pair of ripped jeans that hugged every one of her curves, and a fitted gray t-shirt. It wasn't the outfit, it was the way she was wearing the hell out of it.

"What? You said wear jeans... it's a barbeque." Farren had no idea how sexy she was. Jones was going to have to keep his brothers from staring at his woman all day. Especially his youngest brother, Jasper.

"You look perfect. You're just so damn sexy. How do you expect me to be a gentleman when all I want to do..."

"Don't you dare finish that sentence." Farren held up a manicured hand. "If you get to talkin' dirty, then we'll have to have sex, and you know you don't know how to be quick..."

"I can be quick," Jones interrupted.

Farren narrowed her eyes at him, and he gave her his most charming smile. "No. I won't be late meeting your *entire* family for the first time."

"So you want me to suffer. You know once you turn me on, I have to have it."

"You're not going to suffer, Red. Stop being dramatic." Farren slapped at his chest, and he pulled her in for a kiss.

"You know I love you right?" Jones asked as he looked deep into her honey brown eyes.

"I know. You know I love you too, right?" Farren asked him in return.

"Yeah. But you're going to pay for that 'Red' shit. You know that too... right?" He smiled wickedly.

"Ummm. I sure hope so." Farren winked as she kissed him with a passion that made him fall in love with her all over again.

The End

CPSIA information can be obtained
at www.ICGtesting.com
Printed in the USA
LVHW051948191120
672183LV00015B/2437

9 781983 401589